The mountain lion left the ground in a long leap just as Jonse pulled the trigger. It smashed into him, knocking him backwards. Jonse fell to the ground with the lion on top of him. He heard its snarling, and the moisture from the spitting mouth sprayed his face. Each movement of those massive forequarters twisted Jonse on the ground. Each one of those ripping blows mauled and pummeled his body, but oddly enough he felt no searing pain. The hand holding the pistol was pinned under his body, but he managed to work the hand free. He placed the muzzle against the lion's head and fired. Jonse could feel no lessening of the lion's fury. He kept jerking the trigger until the gun was empty.

Jonse tried to push at the lion's weight with his hands, but he couldn't budge it. The pain was starting now. It shot through the blackness with vivid red flashes, locking his teeth in agony.

The last resistance rushed out of him, and Jonse fell limply back against the ground. It would be a relief to let the blackness have him.

A TIME FOR VENGEANCE

by

GILES A. LUTZ

C

CHARTER BOOKS, NEW YORK

All characters in this book are fictitious.
Any resemblance to actual persons, living or dead,
is purely coincidental.

A TIME FOR VENGEANCE

A Charter Book / published by arrangement with
the author

PRINTING HISTORY
Charter edition / May 1977
Fifth printing / October 1986

ISBN: 0-441-81134-5

Charter Books are published by The Berkley Publishing Group,
200 Madison Avenue, New York, New York 10016.
PRINTED IN THE UNITED STATES OF AMERICA

CHAPTER ONE

JONSE KIRBY SHIVERED as the wind took a fresh bite at him. New Mexico was high country, and Jonse was learning fast that the cold came early here despite what the calendar said.

"Shouldn't be this time of year, Cribber," he said. "It's only mid-October."

The only living thing within sound of his normal speaking voice was the chestnut gelding he rode. In the lonely stretches Jonse had fallen into the habit of talking to Cribber. It passed the time and eased the loneliness.

"What do you think about it, Cribber?"

The gelding flicked his ears forward and back, then snorted lustily.

Jonse nodded judiciously. That sounded like a protest to him. He leaned over and patted the gelding's neck. "Rough country, boy. But maybe we'll be back home one of these days."

The word "home" lodged that familiar lump in Jonse's throat. He swallowed hard to put the lump under control. He didn't have a home any more. All that was destroyed that hot September afternoon. How many times had he cursed himself for being away from the house for just that short time?

He wrenched his thoughts from that agonizing moment and thought about the present. Maybe Cribber wasn't actually protesting, but Jonse was. He wished to God he'd had enough brains to bring a sheepskin coat with him. But Texas had been warm when he left it over a month ago, and he certainly didn't expect this trail to lead him so far. He really hadn't taken time to make preparations of any kind. Blind with rage and grief, Jonse's only desire was to get his hands on the man who killed Marcia. Maybe he would find ease and a mournful consolation one of these days, but right now he was a long way from either.

Jonse hawked and spit to ease his throat. He thought he would run the killer down in a week, or two at the most. Jonse winced as he reflected upon how wrong he had been. The trouble was that he didn't have a name, nor a very good description of the man he wanted. All he had was a hatred that burned deeper with each passing day. It affected his sleeping hours too, breaking through the sodden exhaustion that induced slumber, finally jerking him erect. He would awaken with his heart pounding furiously, and he felt as though he were choking for air. Then he had the long endless struggle to get back to sleep.

Jonse's eyes were bleak as he muttered, "maybe we'll catch up with him tomorrow, Cribber, or the next day."

Right now, the words were only an empty promise,

but it was the only thing that kept him going. He guessed you could kill a man only once, but if he had his say so, he would make it a thousand times, each time slowly and painfully.

Cribber snorted again, and Jonse said, "Talking to myself, Cribber."

Jonse's affection for the horse was evident in his tone. Of all the horses he had seen in his life, he had never looked at an odder one. Jonse would never forget his disbelief when he first laid eyes on Cribber. He had stood, looking at the new foal, saying over and over, "It can't be. It just isn't so."

Jonse had chosen an outstanding brood mare and bred her to the finest stallion he could afford. If this was the result of fine, selective breeding, Jonse thought he would be just as well off to shut his eyes when he made his selection.

All foals were awkward and ungainly when they were first born, their joints looking too big for their size, but Cribber abused that privilege. The older he got, the uglier he grew. Cribber was ewe-necked and hammerheaded. He was all angles, seemingly thrown together by a careless hand, and on top of that he was moon-eyed in one eye. Neighbors used to stop by just for another amused look at him. Jonse had taken a lot of derision directed against his new foal, including the suggestion to just shoot the foal and put him out of his misery.

Jonse hadn't listened to any of those suggestions. In truth, he was fascinated by the ungainly thing cavorting about in the pasture beside his mother. Jonse must have commented a hundred times, "Don't see how your mammy stands you." But the brood mare accepted the colt, and if she could, Jonse guessed he could do no less.

Cribber hadn't smoothed out any as he grew. Jonse couldn't allow him around the barn, for fear the colt would eat it down. Most horses nibbled at wood, but Cribber went far beyond that. Jones swore Cribber must have been sired by a termite. In fact, his penchant for chewing on wood had suggested a logical name for him.

In the three years that followed, Jonse found he had a jewel on his hands. Many times, he wished he hadn't gelded Cribber, but that was done with now.

Jonse broke Cribber when he was two years old, knowing that it was wasted effort. Cribber was the easiest horse he had ever broken. Cribber showed a little surprise, but that was about all.

"Not even any fight in you," Jonse growled as he dismounted.

But he kept on riding Cribber, and his astonishment continued to grow. Cribber might be all angles and bumps, but his disposition alone endeared him to Jonse. Jonse couldn't take a step out of the house without hearing Cribber trumpeting a welcome to him. From then on, Cribber dodged every step Jonse took about the place.

"You're a damned nuisance," Jonse repeatedly growled at him, but he wouldn't have taken anything for the colt. Despite his looks, Cribber had endurance and heart, and there was speed in those awkward strides.

"I was dead wrong about you," Jonse ruefully admitted. "You could be the best horse I'll ever own. Well, one good thing. No horse thief would ever steal you."

Each time Cribber approached, Jonse threw up his

hands to protect his hat. If he didn't, Cribber would pick his hat off his head and drop it on the ground. "Damned nuisance," Jonse said each time he retrieved his hat. "I sure named you wrong."

He reached over and patted Cribber again. Those big, floppy ears twitched in appreciation. "Got to think about making camp soon, Cribber," he said. "We'll stop as soon as I can find a decent patch of grass for you."

"Streak," Jonse yelled. "You get on back here." He stood in the stirrups and looked all around him. That dog had been gone a good twenty minutes. He always came back, but just the same, when his absences were prolonged Jonse fretted over him. Streak was three years old, and Jonse wouldn't have taken anything for him. That hurting lump was back in his throat again. Streak had been Marcia's dog, raised by her from a puppy. Jonse couldn't have gone off and left him, though he had been concerned about taking him along, for he didn't know how long the search would last. He had to take Streak with him, for in some unaccountable way, the dog knew that Marcia was gone forever. Jonse thought that going away and leaving Streak would just about finish him. His worry about Streak being able to stand the traveling faded with each passing day. That dog was made of rawhide. Like Cribber, Streak had heart and endurance, though this morning, Jonse noticed the pads of his paws looked worn. It wasn't surprising the way Streak ran them off. He was an insatiable hunter, looking into every hole, every niche. This was another animal well named because of his speed. Jonse's throat tightened as he remembered Marcia saying, "He goes like a streak, Jonse."

Jonse had smiled at her and replied, "You just named him, Marcia. His name is Streak."

"Streak," Jonse yelled again. He caught a tawny flash of motion off to his left and settled back into his saddle. Streak had heard him and was coming. If small game was plentiful enough, the dog could feed himself. But the last week the hunting had been poor.

"Damned country," Jonse muttered. He knew only one thing for certain. He better find a town and restock soon. There were only a couple of cans of beans in his saddlebags, and about a quarter pound of bacon that was close to turning rancid. This was a hell of a spot to be caught in with winter coming on. Coming too soon, Jonse thought. This morning he found skim ice on the little potholes of water. Yes, he was running short on everything but patience. He would never run out of that until he caught up with his quarry.

Jonse watched Streak run toward him. His pads weren't too sore yet, Jonse thought absently. At first glance, a casual observer would think he was watching a wolf. That long, pointed muzzle and the spikelike ears certainly gave that impression.

Jonse knew from experience what was coming, and he braced himself. Streak left the ground in one fluid, leaping motion, and Jonse caught him.

"Fool dog," he said affectionately. He had a fool dog and a fool horse on his hands. Cribber was used to Streak's jumping on Jonse, for he never turned a hair. Streak was lucky that Cribber had such a placid disposition. An ordinary horse would have tried to kick Streak's head off.

Jonse roughed up Streak's ears while Streak tried to lick his face.

"Stop it, you damned idiot," Jonse complained. His throat was constricting again. It always did when he looked at Streak. He was Marcia's dog, and Jonse was lucky to have him turn so readily to him. He often wondered if there were any memory of Marcia remaining in Streak. At first, Jonse was certain that the dog grieved, for Streak was subdued the first week, and he whined incessantly. Now, it was beginning to look as though all memory of Marcia were fading. If so, Streak was luckier than Jonse would ever be.

He ran his hands over Streak's ribs, feeling how sharply defined they were becoming. "It's been poor hunting, hasn't it, boy?" he asked.

Streak barked several times, and Jonse was positive Streak was making voluble agreement.

"Maybe we'll see something," he said. Tonight, he could give Streak the remainder of the bacon. It wouldn't go far in filling that void that was Streak's stomach, and it would leave Jonse only the beans. He shrugged at the thought. He had lived on beans alone before.

He tossed Streak to the ground. The last three days, Jonse had kept an alert eye out, both for the trail of the man he was following and for something to shoot for Streak. He had come up with a double negative. Either the approaching cold weather had driven all game to lower country, or this land was poor habitation for game to begin with. His sigh took the place of the oath he ordinarily used on this country. He stared bleakly out over the big, empty land, wondering how people made a living here. Whatever that living was had to be sparse, for it had been almost a week since he had seen or talked to anybody. The few people Jonse had met were Mexican, and Jonse was fortunate to have enough Spanish at his command to carry on a halting conversation. Most of them shook their heads at his questions, but one cantina owner had said, "Sí, Señor. I saw such a man. Three or four days ago. Tall and thin with hair as red as the flame of a fire. Sí, he had a bad scar, running from his eye to the point of his chin."

But that information had been almost a week ago. Still, it had been enough of a signpost to keep Jonse headed in this direction. Did the scarred stranger know Jonse was on his trail? It looked that way, Jonse thought grimly. He had one small consolation. This country was just as rough and ungiving to the man he pursued.

Streak ran around Cribber several times, barking his fool head off. He stopped and rubbed noses with Cribber before he took off again. There was a strong bond between the two which was often expressed. That hurting lump was back in Jonse's throat again. He had been perfectly content with his life.

Jonse lifted Cribber's reins to move him on. Thank God, he was beginning to get out of the mountains, for the terrain was smoothing out. That little valley below him looked promising for grass for Cribber. He certainly couldn't expect to find any on this rocky slope.

He let Cribber pick his slow, methodical way. Cribber was as surefooted as a mountain goat. Jonse didn't have to worry about him stumbling or falling.

Blurred motion a good hundred and fifty yards ahead of him caught Jonse's attention, then the motion stopped suddenly. Jonse patiently searched the terrain. He wasn't imagining things. There was something out there; it was small, and it could be a jackrabbit. The ears were too long for an ordinary cottontail. He was glad Streak hadn't seen the animal, or he would be off in a mad chase. Streak could easily run down a cottontail, but even his speed wasn't equal to a jackrabbit's.

Several minutes passed while Jonse's eyes went over every detail of the spot where he thought the motion stopped. He was beginning to believe his eyes were tricking him, then he saw an object crouched beside a boulder. There was too much white to blend in well against the darker color of the rock.

Jonse cautiously eased his rifle out of its scabbard. He could hit a sitting rabbit; he had no doubt of that, but one shot would be all he would be allowed. He was expert with rifle and pistol, but that didn't include hitting a running jackrabbit.

Streak was casting about to Jonse's right, and Jonse prayed, Just stay there. He didn't have to be concerned about Cribber moving. Cribber would hold until he was told to move.

Jonse snugged the rifle butt to his shoulder, took a deep breath, and held it. His and Streak's supper depended upon how good his aim was.

He squeezed the trigger, and that white-gray object jumped straight up into the air. It fell back to flop convulsively on the ground. Its flopping stopped as Jonse watched.

Streak stopped at the rifle's report, his head swiveling in all directions. So far, he hadn't see what Jonse's target was. It was better this way, for Jonse wouldn't be able to reach the rabbit before Streak did. Streak's powerful jaws would tear the rabbit to pieces in a few slashes. Jonse wanted part of that rabbit.

Jonse put away the rifle and grinned at Streak. "Looks like we just got ourselves supper, boy."

Streak's head never stopped swiveling, and his whining had an eager sound. While he still hadn't seen the rabbit, Jonse's tone told him that something had happened.

Jonse urged Cribber toward the small inanimate object on the ground. Streak's nose wasn't too keen, but his eyesight was sharp. Jonse would have to dash the last few remaining yards to get to the rabbit before Streak did.

CHAPTER TWO

JONSE SPURRED Cribber toward the dead rabbit. He swung down and picked it up. This was a hefty one, and it was probably old and tough.

He snatched the rabbit out of Streak's reach. "You can wait a little while," he said sternly. The click of Streak's teeth as he missed his snap at the carcass told Jonse how hungry he was. Ordinarily, Streak was good-mannered dog.

Jonse climbed back into the saddle and, holding the carcass well away from Streak's leap, rode on down into the valley. He nodded with satisfaction as the grass thickened. Cribber was going to have a good meal, too.

Jonse had to rebuke Streak sharply as he skinned and gutted the rabbit. He let Streak have the intestines, and a gulp disposed of them. It was poor fare, but Streak was too hungry to be particular.

It was awkward getting a fire started, for Jonse had to gather the sticks with one hand, and hold the carcass with the other. He had to keep an alert eye on

Streak, for the dog never left his heels, only waiting for a chance to snap at the carcass Jonse carried.

"You don't have a damned manner left," Jonse rebuked him. "You grab this out of my hand, and I'll knock some manners into you." Maybe he could forgive Streak this time, for the dog was hungry.

He got the fire started, then moved Cribber a hundred yards away where the grass was fairly good. At least, Cribber would have a full belly tonight. Upon second thought, Jonse hobbled the gelding. He didn't want Cribber wandering off in a strange country.

The fire was going good when Jonse returned. He cut a thick limb off a bush and tested its capacity to hold the weight of the carcass. Roasting was the only way he had of cooking the rabbit, and he doubted even that would make the meat palatable. He had never heard of any way to cook an old, tough jackrabbit that would make it fit to eat. He shrugged away the doubts. It couldn't turn out too badly. Streak would eat anything.

He skewered the carcass on the stick and held it over the flames, turning it constantly. Jonse heard the sizzle as each drop of fat dropped onto the fire, and the flames momentarily leaped higher. He sniffed at the aroma as the meat turned a slow brown. He didn't know how it would taste, but it smelled good.

The weight of the carcass was a drag on an extended arm, and Jonse shifted it from hand to hand. Streak sat beside him, going quietly crazy with excitement. He whined deep in his throat and slavered at the mouth.

"I want some of this, too," Jonse admonished

Streak. "It won't come off the fire until I can eat some, too."

He shifted the weight to his left hand and turned the rabbit slowly. His face was partially turned from the heat of the fire, and he couldn't stop his thoughts from going back to that horror-filled day when he entered the kitchen to find Marcia lying on the floor. He was quite sure his heart stopped at the sight of the blood, and he was certain she was dead.

"Marcia," he cried brokenly and dropped to his knees beside her. He couldn't believe the miracle, but it was happening, for her eyes fluttered, then opened.

"Jonse," she whispered. "I prayed you would come. I didn't know how long I could hold on."

"Everything's going to be all right," he assured her. "I'll get you in to Doc—"

He stopped in fear as she shook her head. When she spoke, her voice was fainter. "Too late, Jonse. I've known it for some time. But I had to tell you what happened."

He tried to stop her from talking, but there was tremendous determination in that feeble spark of life.

"He was in the house when I came in, Jonse."

Jonse bent closer to hear that fading voice. "He was stealing whatever he could get his hands on, Jonse." She coughed, then stopped, and he was afraid she was gone.

But that determination still remained, and it forced her on. "I screamed at him, Jonse. He pulled out a knife before I knew what he was doing. He stabbed me."

Her eyes closed again, and Jonse knew that too familiar stab of fear again. "Marcia," he said hoarsely. "Who was he, what did he look like?"

Jonse held his ear close to Marcia's mouth to be able to hear those faint, reedy sounds. "A stranger, Jonse. Tall and thin. Redheaded with a long scar on his right cheek. I hope you find him, Jonse." She tried to smile at him, but her strength and determination were fading.

"I will, Marcia," he promised her. He doubted she even heard him, for she sagged in his arms and died.

Jonse didn't know how long he sat there, rocking back and forth, as he tried to force some sanity back into his crazed thoughts. For five years they had been married, and each morning when Jonse awakened beside her, his wonder at her accepting him grew stronger each day. She was small, compared to his bulk, and her laughing eyes and that constant smile was in marked contrast to his usual sober mien. Her sunny disposition eased the problems of daily living. She was Jonse's reason for living. Now she was dead, killed by a petty thief, startled as he ransacked what he thought was an empty house. Two questions hammered repeatedly at Jonse's mind; why did Marcia have to pick that exact moment to return to the house; why did the stranger pick this house to rob? Jonse knew those two whys would torment him forever, for there were no answers to them.

Jonse had no idea of how long he sat there, but it seemed like a racking eternity. He only knew that he had aged, for all the youth had been hammered out of him in that interval.

He carried Marcia out to the buckboard and drove to town. He stopped before Simmon's undertaking parlor where Simmons gave him his professional smile of greeting.

"What's on your mind, Jonse?" Simmons stared at that gray, drawn countenance, and his jaw sagged. "Something bad's happened." He barely managed to get the words out.

"I brought Marcia in, Clyde. She's out in the buckboard. "I want her buried right away."

"My God, what happened?" Simmons gasped.

"Stabbed by a goddamned thief," Jonse said harshly. He could waste no more time on explanations. "I'll be back in a little while. I'll appreciate you doing everything you can."

Simmons wanted to ask more questions, but Jonse cut him short. He had no time to waste in satisfying Simmon's curiosity. He had to find a redheaded man with a scar on one cheek.

Simmons was still babbling when Jonse left the place.

Jonse went methodically about town, asking if anybody had seen a stranger. He was beginning to believe that the man had never stopped in town when he got his first encouraging news. He walked into Arny's saloon, and Arny nodded affirmatively at Jonse's questions.

"I saw that one, Jonse. Fairly early this morning. He had a couple of beers and left. It looked like he was scraping the bottom of his pockets to pay for them."

"Thanks, Arny," Jonse said in a dead voice. Now, where did he start looking for this man?

The sheriff's office was directly across the street, and after a moment's thought, Jonse crossed to it. Haskill was a good sheriff. He had more than earned the privilege of being informed about what was going on.

Ord Plummer was in the office with Haskill when Jonse entered. His face was flushed with indignation, and he broke his harangue at Haskill only long enough to nod to Jonse.

"Goddamn it, Pat," Plummer said hotly. "I know it was him. I fed the bastard breakfast. He thanked me, then said he guessed he'd be moving on."

His words were jamming together, and he took a deep breath to slow them down. "An hour later, my best horse was gone."

"Do you think this stranger took him?" Haskill asked.

"Had to," Plummer said positively. "Nobody else around who would have done it."

"Was this stranger redheaded and with a scar on his face?" Jonse asked.

Plummer's eyes widened. "You saw him, too?"

Jonse felt the moisture well up into his eyes, and he was afraid he would break down and bawl before these two. He gulped hard and managed to say, "I didn't see him. But he killed Marcia. Stabbed her. She caught him while he was robbing our house."

"My God, Jonse," Haskill said in shock. "How long ago?"

"I don't know," Jonse said dully. He didn't know how much time slipped away while he held Marcia.

Haskill bounded to his feet. "Which way did he go, Ord?"

Plummer threw up his hands helplessly. "How do I know?" he growled. He was still stunned by Jonse's announcement. "Jesus, I'm sorry, Jonse."

Jonse was beginning to throw off his grief-induced lethargy. He needed action to keep from thinking.

"Have you got any idea which way he could have gone, Ord?"

Plummer shook his head, then his expression lightened. "He took my Rusty horse. You know him, Jonse. Caulkings built up his left front shoe to balance his stride."

Jonse nodded. He knew the horse well. Rusty left a distinctive track. At least that was something to go on.

"Ready to go, Jonse?" Haskill asked.

"I'm ready," Jonse said grimly. "Oh damn it." His voice was furious. "I brought Marcia in in the buckboard. I haven't got a horse."

Plummer solved that dilemma in a hurry, for he said, "Take my horse, Jonse. I'd rather you catch the son of a bitch than me. I hope to God you do."

Jonse started to nod his appreciation, then stopped. "That leaves you afoot, Ord. How will you—"

Plummer cut him short. "I'll manage, Jonse. Don't give me a second thought.

Jonse nodded his thanks and walked out behind Haskill. Haskill's horse was tied alongside of Plummer's roan. Jonse was grateful for the loan of the horse, but he wished to God he had Cribber with him.

"We'd better ride out to Plummer's and see if we can pick up a track there," Haskill suggested.

Jonse nodded impatiently. That would take time, but there was no other course left open to him.

"Lucky I didn't leave Swamper at the stable when I came in this morning," Haskill commented.

Jonse flashed Haskill a savage look. He was in no mood for conversation.

Plummer's place was five miles west of town. Jonse wondered if the stranger stole the horse before or after he killed Marcia. Jonse wiped all speculations from his mind. It didn't matter one way or the other. He would find Marcia's killer.

It had been dry the last few weeks, and dust lay thick on the ground. Jonse spotted Rusty's distinctive track before he reached Plummer's corral. He pointed it out to Haskill. The tracks led due west and had been made some time ago, for the breeze was strong enough to crumble the clear outlines. In places, the breeze had been a broom, sweeping the tracks clean. By the length of Rusty's strides, the stranger was riding hard. That didn't matter, either. He couldn't run fast nor far enough to get away.

In long stretches, the tracks were completely gone, but Jonse pressed on. He would worry about the lack of tracks when he came to a crossroad. It was doubtful the stranger would leave a main road and cross open country.

A mile up ahead, Jonse had to make a decision, for he came to a crossroad. He got down and cast about, losing more precious time. Jonse covered the crossroad several hundred yards in both directions before he was satisfied Rusty hadn't turned either way.

He came back and remounted. "Looks like he didn't leave this road," he said.

"Good," Haskill said flatly. "Maybe we can start gaining a little on him."

Jonse didn't think so, though he didn't voice his doubt. He was strung tight until he saw another familiar track a quarter of a mile further on. He didn't have much to go on, only a general description of the man and the horse he was riding, and he had a general direction. Those where pretty skimpy clues to start with, but he would have to make them do. But it was going to be a slow, tedious chase. That wasn't what was driving Jonse at the moment. He had left Marcia back in town. Jonse couldn't start his driving search until he had taken care of Marcia.

He pulled up, and Haskill looked questioningly at him. "Ben, I left Marcia with Simmons. I can't leave her alone."

Haskill's mouth opened, then snapped shut, and he nodded his understanding. "Sure," he said.

"Running him down is going to take time, Ben," Jonse said somberly. "More time than you can afford to spend away from your office."

Haskill's mouth opened again, but before he could speak, Jonse said, "I'm talking about a lot of time, Ben. It could be weeks." His eyes bored into Haskill. "Are you ready to spend that much time on the trail?"

Indecision weakened Haskill's face, and Jonse said, "I am. I'm ready to go just as far as he takes me. But I want to take care of Marcia, then get Cribber. I've got a feeling I'll need him before I'm through."

Jonse saw the arguments gather on Haskill's face, and he stilled them with a savage slash of his hand. "I know what has to be done, Ben."

Haskill sighed as the indecision left his face. "Sure, you do, Jonse. But I'm going on a little farther. I might get lucky and get a definite lead."

Jonse whirled Plummer's horse, lifting his hand in a wave to Haskill. He hoped to God Haskill was right, but he couldn't still the doubt that filled him. The cold feeling that Haskill wouldn't catch up with the man was a solid lump of misery in his belly. Haskill would do everything he could, but he didn't have the one thing he needed most. That was patience. That was about all he had left, Jonse thought bleakly. He would drive that redheaded killer as far as necessary, even if it meant driving him into the ocean. Jonse had another ingredient to add to that patience; an unwavering determination.

Simmons had made the necessary arrangements, for he nodded to Jonse as he walked into the office. "Any particular place you want to bury her, Jonse?"

"The town cemetery," Jonse said woodenly. Maybe Marcia would have preferred to be buried on their own land, but that would take more time. Jonse was too hard-driven to feel he had the time. Jonse silently begged for Marcia's understanding.

At the funeral Jonse said his final goodbye to Marcia. His face was a block of granite as he listened to the preacher's words, but he couldn't have told anybody their meaning. Only a dozen people attended the service, for the news of Marcia's death hadn't time to spread far.

After the service, Jonse had to stop and listen to people's awkward attempt at consolation. He patiently endured them, though his impatience was screaming at him. Everybody meant well, and Marcia was liked by everyone. But none of this would bring her back, and it was stopping Jonse from getting on with a job.

He got away as quickly as he could, drove back to his place, and saddled Cribber. Streak joined him, and there was a mournful note to his whining. Streak hadn't been around when Marcia died, but with an animal's instinct, he knew something was definitely wrong.

Jonse didn't hesitate for a moment. "Come on, boy," he said. Streak wouldn't stay around with both Jonse and Marcia gone. He would wander the country over, trying to find them, and Jonse didn't want that.

Jonse hated to enter that house again. No matter how he tried to keep his eyes from the dried bloodstain on the floor, he knew it was there, and his eyes kept straying to it. Each time, he thought he would choke on the poisonous rage that enveloped him. He would give everything he owned, or ever hoped to own for just a minute or two with Marcia's killer.

He gathered up a few cans of food in the kitchen and dropped them into a bag. That would keep him from losing time stopping for groceries in town. What came after the supplies ran out, he didn't know. He would have to depend on living off the land.

In the bedroom, the sight of the empty bed almost broke him up. He jerked his eyes from it and got a clean shirt and two pairs of socks from a drawer. Jonse shook his head as he turned to leave the room. He would never spend a tougher few minutes.

Going back into the kitchen, he picked up his cartridge belt and pistol and strapped them on. His hand closed on his favorite rifle from the gun rack. Adding a fresh box of shells to his supplies made him as ready as he could ever be.

He mounted Cribber and led Plummer's horse, as he turned toward Plummer's. He would have to leave the horse there. Streak fell into that easy loping run of his. Could Streak stand day after day of this? That was another unanswered question. Only time would tell.

Jonse was well into the following day when he saw two small, indistinct figures coming down the road toward him. He stood in the stirrups and shaded his eyes against the western sun. The distance and the glare made it difficult for him to determine what those figures were, then he finally decided it was a man, leading a horse.

Jonse's jaw was set hard as he settled back into the saddle. He didn't know who those figures were, but he had the cold feeling that their appearance didn't augur well for him.

He touched Cribber with the spurs, asking for and getting speed. He had covered only half the intervening distance when he saw who those figures were. That was Haskill, leading Swamper. That was more wrath than physical distress on Haskill's face.

Jonse reached him, pulled up, and asked, "What happened, Ben?"

Haskill had to get a stream of obscenities out of his system before he could answer. He gestured at the horse and said bitterly, "Swamper went lame a couple of hours ago."

Jonse had the same inclination to swear, and he throttled the impulse. Everything had gone against him so far.

"Did you ever catch a look at him, Ben?"

Haskill shook his head. "Not a glimmer. But I thought the tracks were getting a little fresher."

That was only the sorriest of consolations. Jonse wanted to beat at something with his hands to ease the mounting rage. He had no idea how far he was behind the man he wanted, but Swamper going lame had added considerable margin to the stranger's advantage.

Now he was faced with another dilemma. Haskill was out here afoot. Jonse groaned as he thought of how long it would take getting Haskill back to town.

Haskill guessed at the thoughts churning in Jonse's head, for he said quietly, "I want you to go ahead, Jonse." At the stubbornness forming in Jonse's face, he said violently, "Goddamn it, I've walked a piece before. You've already lost enough time."

Jonse made his decision. "You're sure you'll be all right?"

Haskill managed a wan grin. "Slow but all right. Is there anything I can do for you, Jonse?"

"Ask some of my neighbors to look out for things on my place. I don't know when I'll get back."

"They'll be glad to do that, Jonse." Haskill looked at Streak, sitting to one side of them, his tongue lolling out. "You won't make much time with him."

Jonse knew that it wasn't speed that was paramount now; just endurance and a determination that couldn't be weakened. He had both of those qualities in abundance.

"He'll make it, Ben."

Haskill's sigh was a long doleful sound, expressing his doubt. "I wish you all the luck in the world, Jonse."

"I know," Jonse said somberly. All his luck had run out with Marcia's death. He raised a hand in a salute and urged Cribber into a canter.

He looked back after a couple of hundred yards. Haskill trudged toward town. Maybe somebody else would come along and give him a lift. Jonse hoped so, then turned his thoughts from Haskill. He had one thing on his mind that crushed out all other considerations.

Streak whined and rubbed against Jonse, jerking him back from the desolute memories of the past. Jonse looked at the carcass of the rabbit. Those thoughts had flooded in, erasing all thought of the present. One side of the carcass was pretty thoroughly charred.

Jonse turned the stick. "Just about burned it up, didn't I, boy?"

Maybe Streak sensed the meat was burning, or perhaps he sensed the agony Jonse was going through. Jonse preferred to think it was the latter.

"Almost done, Streak," he said. He watched the roasting carcass intently. He had come a long way with no real tangible signs of success. Long ago, he had lost Rusty's tracks. Now all he could do was to stop at every habitation, every town, to make his persistent inquiries. Too many of the answers had been negative. But every now and then, he heard a definite word that told him he wasn't chasing a will-o'-the-wisp. A few people had seen the stranger passing through, remembering the flame of his hair and the outstanding scar on his face. The man existed, and Jonse was still behind him. Each time he received an affirmative word, his hope rekindled. He still hadn't heard a name to hang on the man, but he existed. He was somewhere ahead of Jonse, and by his actions still running hard. How far ahead, Jonse didn't know. He wouldn't allow himself to think of how much distance remained between them. He had no choice; all he could do was to keep on until he caught up with the redheaded man.

Jonse sat hunched over, a big, bluff man staring fixedly at the fire, occasionally turning the meat. He was unbelievably homely, his face looking as craggy as an outcropping of granite. His smile changed everything, giving a new warmth to his face, his eyes. But since Marcia died, he had no reason to smile. He had an insatiable appetite for work, and he had carved out his small ranch through hard work and application. Both of his parents had the same aptitude, and he guessed he inherited that trait from them. Both of them died when he was sixteen within months of each other. Jones thought he learned then the meaning of loneliness, but it was nothing compared to what he felt now.

He had bent doggedly to each day's chores, not letting himself think ahead. Everything changed when he met Marcia. Just looking at her explained all the reasons why he had plowed doggedly ahead. He never lost that original awe that she could ever be interested in him. But she had been. She had—

Jonse stirred and put a hard hand on such thoughts. He couldn't go on the rest of his life, wracking himself like this. He supposed that only the passage of time would bring relief, but so far there hadn't been enough elapsed time to accomplish much along that line.

His head whipped around as he heard the scream, and for a moment, he was frozen. That scream sounded like a woman in torment, and that wasn't possible. This was empty country. No woman would be out here.

He heard the scream again, and his face cleared. That was the doleful wail of a hunting painter, sound-

25

ing alarmingly like a woman in distress.

"Mountain lion, Streak," he muttered. He sure didn't want Streak tangling with something like that. From the sparseness of the game, Jonse thought that was a starving lion. "Probably as hungry as we are," he said aloud.

Jonse stared into the darkness, an unease growing within him. He wished he could tell by the sound how far that lion was from him. He needed some answers to quiet his uneasiness; how fast was that lion traveling and in which direction was he headed?

Jonse withdrew the stick from the fire and inspected the carcass. A poor job of roasting, he thought critically. One side of the meat was overdone, the other side needed more roasting. "I guess we'll go ahead and eat, Streak."

Streak quivered with eagerness, and the saliva dropped from his jaws.

CHAPTER THREE

"HOLD IT, BOY," Jones commanded. "You don't think you're going to get all of this, do you?"

His head lifted as he heard the scream again. That sounded farther away. He pulled his knife from its sheath and severed a hind leg from the rabbit. "Cuts tough, too," he muttered.

He tossed the remainder of the carcass to Streak with the warning, "Watch yourself. It's hot."

Streak grabbed up the meat, shook his head, and dropped it.

Jonse shook his head. "You never listen, do you?"

Streak's belly must be setting up a clamor that he couldn't ignore, for he grabbed up the carcass again.

Jonse shrugged. "It's your tongue," he said.

All of his earlier estimations of this meat proved to be correct. It was tough and stringy. Jonse chewed the bite thoroughly before he could get it down.

He scowled and said, "No taste. I'm not that hungry." He tossed the leg to Streak.

If Streak had any complaints about the meat, it

didn't show. He anchored the carcass down with his paws and ripped off chunk after chunk.

A faint grin moved Jonse's lips. "It's a good thing one of us isn't particular," he commented.

He pulled a can of beans out of one of the saddlebags. Scraping a hole in the fire, he set the can down into the flames. He didn't wait long, not wanting that can to get too hot to handle.

With a stick, he knocked the can away from the fire, rolling the can about on the ground with his foot. He grunted as he gingerly picked it up. Still hot, but he could manage.

With a knife blade, Jonse sawed open the lid of the can, his face set with dissapproval as he did so. That was damned rough treatment for a good blade.

After eating half of the beans, Jonse emptied the remainder out before Streak. The beans were all right. He simply wasn't as hungry as he thought he was.

Streak furiously waggled his tail in appreciation. He didn't care what the food was, or what it tasted like as long as it filled up that empty void below those avid jaws.

"You'd eat anything," Jonse said as he watched Streak gulp down bite after bite so rapidly, Jonse was sure he couldn't taste them. Maybe Streak had a taster in his belly.

Jonse jerked as he heard that scream again. That sounded much closer than the last scream, and Jones's worry immediately centered on Cribber. Hobbled the way the gelding was, Cribber could do little to defend himself. He wasn't even able to move very far, and he had no speed.

Jonse hurried over to where his saddle lay and

jerked the rifle from its scabbard. He was going to move Cribber closer to the camp, and even that wouldn't erase all his worry about him, not as long as a hungry mountain lion roamed in the vicinity.

Streak lifted his head and whined as he saw Jonse leaving. He wanted to go with Jonse. Most of the meat was gone, but the bones remained, and Streak was reluctant to leave them.

"Wait here," Jonse ordered. "I'll be right back."

A pale, watery moon afforded poor illumination, but Jonse was grateful for even this inadequate light.

His blood froze as he heard the scream again. This time, it was much closer. That damned lion must have caught Cribber's scent and was stalking him.

Cribber sensed the menace too, for he kept moving constantly in little hampered steps, nickering deep in his throat. Twice, he let all his terror out in loud, prolonged bugling.

"Easy," Jonse called to him. "Everything's all right."

Jonse was a good thirty yards from Cribber when he saw the dark form, close to the ground, dashing soundlessly toward Cribber. The lion's speed was appalling. Jonse hardly had time to think about it, let alone get the rifle butt against his shoulder. When he finally exploded into action, it was too late to fire for fear of hitting the horse.

The lion made its spring, and Cribber reared at the same time. Cribber struck with those hobbled front hoofs, and his aim was good. Those hoofs stopped that leaping charge in midair, knocking the lion to the ground.

The cat's snarl rang in Jonse's ears, and he heard Cribber's high-pitched scream, carrying both pain and rage. Cribber whirled, getting between Jonse and the cat, and Jonse saw dark streaks coursing from Cribber's left shoulder. He was sick with worry and fear. That damned cat had gotten in a swipe of his paw that opened Cribber's flesh.

He ran around Cribber, trying to get a clear shot. "Damn you, Cribber," he yelled. "Stand still."

Something whipped by Jonse so fast that for a moment he didn't realize what it was. "No," he screamed at the top of his lungs. "Streak, stay out of this."

It would have done as much good to yell commands at a mountain. A mere voice wasn't going to stop or turn Streak.

The two forms collided and blended into a single, snarling, raging mass of churning, furry bodies. Streak's growling never stopped, and the cat's hissing rage rose above the growling.

Jonse ran toward them, his heart bounding up into his throat. Streak had no chance against that fury incarnate.

Jonse didn't dare risk a shot for fear of hitting Streak. He reversed the rifle, grabbing it by the muzzle as he ran. If he could get just one clear swipe at the cat, he might be able to knock the animal away from Streak.

He danced around, trying to avoid the thrashing mass of enraged animals. Twice, he thought the cat's head was clear, but before he could swing the rifle's stock, the head was gone.

Now, he told himself as the lion's head came into momentary view again. Jonse swung with all the power in his arms, and his aim was good. The rifle butt smashed across the lion's muzzle, the impact so hard that it knocked the rifle from Jonse's hands. The shock of the blow was enough for the cat to let go of Streak and whirl on Jonse. Streak fell to the ground, and he was hurt badly, for a leg buckled under him, as he tried to charge the lion again.

Jonse caught only a glimpse of that snarling, spitting face as he drew his pistol. He had knocked all thought of Streak out of the cat's head, turning its full fury on him. He must have hit a tender spot with that rifle blow, Jonse thought, as he braced himself for the lion's leap. The cat covered the intervening distance with terrifying speed, and it left the ground in a long, ground-covering leap just as Jonse pulled the trigger. He couldn't tell whether or not his shot found its mark. The lion smashed into him, knocking him backwards. Jonse fell to the ground with the lion on top of him. He heard its snarling, and the moisture from the spitting mouth sprayed his face. Each movement of those massive forequarters twisted Jonse on the ground. Jonse knew he was being hurt badly. Each one of those ripping blows mauled and pummeled his body, but oddly enough he felt no searing pain. The hand holding the pistol was pinned under his body, but he managed to work the hand free. He placed the muzzle against the lion's head and fired. Jonse could feel no lessening of the lion's fury. He knew he was getting weaker. Each blow of the cat's paw released a new wave of encroaching blackness, and now it was beginning to rush at him. Jonse's vision was no longer clear, and the nausea in his stomach was spreading, threatening to engulf him. He kept jerking the trigger until the gun was empty.

Jonse tried to push at the lion's weight with his hands, but be couldn't budge it. The pain was starting now. It shot through the blackness with vivid red lashes, locking his teeth in agony.

The last resistance rushed out of him, and Jonse fell limply back against the ground. It would be a relief to let the blackness have him. His last conscious thought was that he was never going to catch up with the man he wanted so badly.

CHAPTER FOUR

JONSE OPENED HIS EYES, but the light was so blinding that it was too painful to endure, and he hastily closed them.

"Ah," a soft voice said. "So you finally decided to return to the world of the living."

Jonse thought about the words without opening his eyes. Those soft tones were undoubtedly a woman's, and while her English was strongly accented, it was good enough to convey her thoughts.

That proposed many questions, and just the effort of thinking about them exhausted Jonse. What was he doing with a Spanish woman, and where was he?

His thoughts were as heavy as a horse's hoofs plowing through a sticky bog. Like the horse lifting a heavy foot before it could struggle on, so were the words in Jonse's stubborn mind. Each one had to be dug out of the clinging mass of a recalcitrant memory. My God! Why was he so tired? The effort of trying to recall just the simplest things left him utterly exhausted.

Jonse opened his eyes again, nerving himself to endure the brutal impact of light that he knew would come. He groaned softly. He was right about that lash of light. He forced his eyes to remain open, even though every instinct wanted to close them and retreat into the comforting blackness.

He stared steadily at the light, and its intensity gradually lessened. What was happening to him? That was only a coal-oil lamp, and its soft light couldn't produce the brutal effect he had first known.

Pain washed over him, as he tried to turn his head. He felt it in every fibre of his body. "Jesus!" The oath escaped him before he could prevent it. Remembering a woman had spoken to him, he mumbled, "I'm sorry." He must have been through something really bad, but he couldn't remember what it was.

"It's all right," the same voice assured him. A light touch rested momentarily on his brow. "Ah, you are better. The fever has broken."

Jonse gritted his teeth against the pain he knew it would bring, but he turned his head to look at the woman. His vision must be faulty, because he couldn't tell much about her. He briefly closed his eyes. When he looked at her again, the hazy outline was still there. She was on the small side; that was about all he could tell.

"Where am I?" he asked hoarsely. "Why am I here?"

She leaned closer to him, and the only clear impression he had of her was those huge brown eyes, liquid wells of compassion.

"*Dios*," she breathed. "You do not remember anything?"

"I try to," he said. "But I can't get a grip on it. Why am I so beaten up? Was I in a fight?"

"A terrible fight," she said earnestly. "It is one of *Dios's* miracles that you are alive. A man does not go up against a mountain lion with only his bare hands."

The breath whooshed out of him as that moment came back, vivid and terrifying. He could even smell the lion's fetid breath.

"Oh, God," Jonse groaned. "My dog and horse."

He struggled to sit up, and a firm hand pressed him back. "Señor, do not fret. They, too, are alive and recovering. My son brought the three of you in."

Jonse was content to sink back. He had gone through a nightmare all right, one that was too terrifyingly real. The weakness and the pain weren't imaginary, either. They too, were far too real.

He lay there, thinking about what the woman said, and her words brought an ease to him and erased the inner struggle. As long as he knew what had happened, he could cope with it. The cessation of the struggle brought on a lassitude that made his eyelids heavy.

"I can't tell you how grateful I am to you and your son," he said drowsily. "I'll be up and out of here in a little bit."

Jonse thought the woman was going to protest, but she said, "Sleep! It is the best thing for you. We have much to talk about later."

Jonse thought he heard a door close, but he couldn't be too sure of that, either. His thoughts were turning heavy again, but that no longer scared him. The lamp said it was still night. He hadn't lost too much time. Just a little more rest, and he could pick up the trail again. He would never listen to any better news than that Cribber and Streak were recovering from their tangle with the cat.

Two voices awakened him in the morning. Jonse opened his eyes and stared vaguely about him. He knew it was morning, for the sun streamed through the small, sparsely furnished room.

"Luis," the woman said sternly to the man beside her. "I told you not to come in here this early. See! You have awakened him."

"Madre, I am sorry," the man said in instant contrition. "I would not have disturbed him for anything in the world. Ever since you told me he spoke clearly for the first time last night. I have been waiting eagerly to talk to the man who could have won such a fight."

He spoke in Spanish, but Jonse was able to follow him fairly well. He was a small man, not much taller than his mother, but Jonse would guess there was a wiriness in that compact frame. His eyes were merry, and the mouth was cut for laughter, though Jonse had the odd feeling that this one hadn't known too many reasons for laughter lately. There seemed to be strain around the eyes, and the lines from the corners of his mouth were cut too deeply. Jonse knew that only two things could put such lines in one so young, fear or worry.

The resemblance between mother and son was strong. Jonse could see her clearly for the first time. Though she was plump, there were remnants of great beauty in her features, though the eyes seemed inordinately sad. Her mouth was soft and facile, ready to change appearance at any change in her mood. Jonse could almost imagine her as a slender young girl with those enormous eyes and a flashing spirit that went with them. Then, she must have turned every male head she passed.

The two started to withdraw, and Jonse stopped them. "Stay," he insisted. "I want to talk to you." His head was clear, the thoughts clean-cut and sharp. "First, I want to thank you for helping me. I'm Jonse Kirby. I was just passing through your country. I had no idea your house was anywhere near. The last thing I remember was that cat jumping on me." He attempted a smile, and even that hurt. He was afraid they were still undecided about staying, and he extended a hand toward them. Another wince crossed his face. Jonse stared at his arm in astonishment. It was wrapped in bandages from shoulder to wrist, and there were two angry scratches on his hand.

"Señor, I am Luis Higuera," the slight figure said eagerly as he bounded forward. He gently took Jonse's hand as though he feared he would break it. "This is my madre, Señora Marita Higuera."

Jonse grinned as he took Luis's hand. "I won't break," he said. "Though for a time last night I wasn't so sure of that."

Luis and his mother exchanged astonished glances. "*Dios*," Luis murmured. "He thinks it happened only last night."

Marita shook her head in pity as she looked at Jonse. "It has been much longer than that, señor."

Jonse felt cold as though an icy wind blew suddenly over him. "I don't understand what you mean," he said in a shaking voice.

Luis started to answer, and Marita checked him with an upraised hand. "I will tell him, Luis. You are too impulsive. It must be told gently."

Jonse looked from mother to son. Good God! What were they trying to tell him? "Are you trying to say something went wrong with my horse and dog?" he asked hoarsely. "But last night, you said—"

Marita's shaking head interrupted him. "They are still fine. Only a short while ago Luis fed them. He came in, beaming all over his face. He said he never saw two animals heal faster."

She hesitated as though she sought the proper words before she could go on. "You are fortunate to be alive, señor. You lost so much blood. There were many times when I despaired of saving you. The fever kept mounting, until I thought my hand would burn when I changed the bandages. I turned to the only thing left me. I asked *Dios* to save you. He heard and answered. For the first time last night, I could see that answer."

Jonse stared incredulously. "Are you trying to tell me I've been here for a long time? How long?"

Marita's voice lowered to almost a whisper. "Very long, señor. For ten days you did not utter a lucid word."

Jonse wanted to shout at her that she was wrong; that it couldn't be. He weighed the enormity of what she said. Ten days! Just thinking about them sickened him. In that much time the trail could become so dim that it could be impossible to ever find it again. He lay there, crushed under the new weight of the problem. In ten days, the stranger could get well out of the state. Which direction would he go? Jonse's rock-hard determination almost weakened. In that length of time people would have forgotten that once a stranger had passed this way. Jonse wanted to curse the magnitude of what he faced. For the first time in his life he felt complete despair.

His jaw hardened. He would not betray a vow he had made to Marcia and himself. The difficulties of accomplishing the vow would take longer; that was all.

Jonse threw the light blanket from him and started to sit up. Just that small effort left him weak and gasping for breath.

"What do you think you are doing?" Marita cried.

Jonse glared at her, then his eyes softened. She didn't realize what he had to do. "I've got to get up," he said simply. "In a moment, this weakness will pass."

For the first time, he realized that he was naked under the blanket. Except for the bandages he wore nothing.

Jonse's face crimsoned, and he hastily pulled the blanket over him. "My clothes are gone," he blurted out. "Who—" He couldn't finish the embarrassing question.

Marita guessed at his torment, for she smiled faintly. "You can accuse me. How did you think I put the bandages on you? Yes, and changed them. Do not distress yourself, señor. I have seen male bodies before. Only you are embarrassed."

Jonse tried to meet her eyes and couldn't. He guessed he was flushing all over, for he could feel the heat in his face and body. Luis tried to keep his face straight, but his lips kept twitching. This must be a subject of much merriment to him.

"I, too, helped, señor," he said. "You were too heavy for her to handle alone."

Jonse lay there and glowered at Luis, but he could feel the heat in his face slowly fading. He tried to chuckle, but it was a thin reedy sound with no real mirth in it.

"I guess it's done now," he admitted. "Haven't been handled like that since I was a baby," he said gruffly.

That released Marita's and Luis's restraint, for they broke into laughter. Luis howled with his mirth, Marita laughed more softly.

Jonse couldn't join in. This wasn't funny to him, but he could endure it.

"Forgive me, señor," Marita begged. "But you were so outraged at the thought of a woman—" She burst into laughter again, breaking up her words.

"I guess I was," Jonse said sheepishly. "I find out I owe you two much more than I thought. From what I saw I've got nothing but bandages on me."

Luis spread his fingers, making claws of them. He swiped the hand through the air. "A mountain lion has wicked claws, señor. He must have used them well before you killed him." He nodded at the question in Jonse's eyes. "Yes, he was dead, lying on top of you when I found you. *Dios.* I have never seen so much blood in my life. I could not tell which was yours and which belonged to the lion.

Jonse winced as that moment came vividly back to him. He knew the lion mauled him but not this badly. "How bad was it?" he asked quietly.

Marita took over the conversation. "Many scratches, señor. Some of them deep; all over your arms and chest. Yes, and many tooth marks. They contributed to a great loss of blood. Even your face is marked."

Jonse lifted a hand and gingerly felt the scabs forming under his beard. "Guess they can't do too much to harm my beauty," he grunted.

"They will heal with hardly a trace," Marita assured him.

Jonse lay there, reflecting upon what the two told him. He could well understand the terrible weakness that insisted upon holding him down.

"How bad were Cribber and Streak?" he asked.

"Señor ," Luis said, then stopped. Why was the Americano frowning at him so?

"I have listened to that title long enough," Jonse said positively. "My friends call me Jonse. I don't know where I'd find two who better fit that classification than you two."

Luis's happy smile lighted his face. "To call you that would be a great honor. Cribber and Streak? They are your horse and dog?"

"Cribber's the gelding," Jonse said.

"An ugly one," Luis said. "But I have seen that kind before. The beauty of them lies beneath that ugliness."

Jonse's eyes glowed. He could like this man. "Cribber never knows when to stop," he said simply. "As for speed I'd match him against anything I ever saw."

Luis nodded in quiet appreciation. "I felt all that, Jonse, whenever I looked at him. He did not resent a stranger handling him. He has a bad slash on his left forequarter. Much worse at first sight than it is. None of the muscles were cut. He heals nicely. I do not think he will lose any of his speed, though I could do little about the scar his injury will leave."

"He's like I am," Jonse said and grinned. "A scar

or two won't hurt his beauty." He couldn't suppress the anxiety behind his words. "Streak's in worse shape?"

Luis nodded soberly, but he hastened to add. "But he, too, will recover. He took a far worse mauling. He is up and hobbling around. But I'm afraid this will cost him some of his natural speed."

Jonse hated to hear that. If Luis was right, this meant Streak could no longer keep up with him.

Jonse looked pointedly at Marita. "I've got to get out and see them. If you'd get my clothes—"

He found out that Marita had a determination that equaled his own. "You will not," she stormed. "Don't you realize how weak you are? Maybe tomorrow or the next day. We will see how you progress."

Luis spread his hands and grinned at Jonse. "You will find that her word is law here. It will do you no good to argue further."

Jonse sighed. He didn't need much movement to convince him that Marita was right.

"Tomorrow, then," he growled. That was another day added to the vast gap that already faced him. "I'm going tomorrow."

"We shall see," Marita replied. "Now the only thing that concerns us is breakfast. You have eaten so little for many days. You should be hungry."

Jonse's stomach rumbled. Hungry was too mild a word. He was ravenous. "I guess I am," he admitted.

"I will bring you something right away," Marita promised. She turned and walked rapidly out of the room.

Jonse's eyes stung with tears at the memory her

movement recalled. Marcia had that same effortless grace. It was odd that their first names were so similar. The stinging grew worse, and Jonse turned his head so that Luis could not see the tears starting.

"Your mother is quite a woman," he said gruffly.

"Yes," Luis said. There was a strained note in the word that jerked Jonse's attention back to Luis. Surely, there could be no disagreement between those two.

"People will not let her alone," Luis said passionately. "They hound her from all sides. I swear I will kill every one of them someday."

Luis ducked his head in embarrassment as his passion was spent. "Forget that," he said stiffly. "It is a family affair." He followed his mother out of the room.

Jonse reflectively looked at the ceiling. So there was some trouble that put the strain and worry in Marita and her son. Though he had been told to stay out of it, maybe he could help when he was stronger. God knew, he owed them far more than just a helping hand. His face twisted in sudden recrimination. Here he had a problem of his own so big that a solution seemed impossible. Here he was thinking of adding another problem to the one he already had.

"Oh, goddamn it," he said in a sudden burst of rage. He lay there, glowering at the ceiling.

CHAPTER FIVE

JONSE LIMPED IN TO THE TABLE with Luis's support. Marita had insisted Jonse wasn't strong enough to get out of bed, but Jonse had overridden her. "If I lay in that bed another minute, you'll have a crazy man on your hands. I couldn't allow that to happen to you."

So Marita had given in, though she watched every uncertain step with anxious eyes. Jonse sank down into his chair and blew out a hard breath. It wasn't possible that just that tiny walk could leave his legs trembling so. He grinned reassuringly at Marita. "I feel great," he lied. "Strong as a bull."

"You disappoint me," she said.

Jonse frowned in perplexity. "Why?"

"I have found too many men are liars," Marita said sternly. "But I did not think you were one of them."

It was the first time in a long stretch of days that Jonse felt like laughing. He let it pour out, then stopped and shook his head. "I should have known I couldn't fool you. I still feel shaky inside." At

Marita's gathering frown, he hastened to add, "But so much better, or I could not have walked this far."

Marita considered that, then said dubiously, "Perhaps not. But you cannot rush the healing. If you try, you will lose in the long run."

Perhaps Marita spoke from wisdom, but she didn't know the pressures on Jonse. If this was a normal time, he might be able to follow her advice. But this wasn't normal, and he had no time to spare.

Jonse changed the subject as an enticing aroma drifted to him. "Is that meat I smell? It seems forever since I had any solid food."

He grinned at Marita to soften his accusation. She had kept him filled with a thin gruel. It was savory enough, but after many such meals a man's stomach rebelled. Jonse wanted something solid to get his teeth into.

Marita's laughter was an amused, light burst of sound. "So you are complaining. That is a sure sign you are much better." Marita looked at Luis. "He brings back all the old days to me, Luis. Do you remember how you complained about the food I set before you when you were growing up?"

Luis grinned. "Too well. But I never won, did I?" Luis seemed more relaxed, happier than when Jonse talked to him this morning. "I finally learned to quit arguing with her. She always knew best."

Marita rose and walked to the oven. She opened the old cast-iron door and pulled out a large, flat pan. Jonse saw the mound of roasted meat, its brown crust telling him it was beautifully done. The aroma was much stronger, filling the kitchen, and the savory smell started the juices flowing in Jonse's mouth.

He could hardly wait to take his first bite. His eyes momentarily closed in bliss. "Only the best I ever tasted. Though I don't recognize what kind of meat it is."

"Roasted leg of lamb," Marita said.

Jonse laid down his knife and fork and looked at the meat on his plate.

"You find something wrong with it?" Marita challenged.

"I tried mutton a couple of times," Jonse explained. "It didn't go down too well. You see, I'm a cattleman." He hoped that made her understand.

"And we are sheep people." A trace of stiffness was in Marita's voice.

Jonse tried to ease the awkward moment. He didn't want her to think he was critical. "It's just an ingrained taste, I guess," he said in embarrassment.

"You liked the first bite," Marita said. Her eyes were snapping. She raised her hand, stopping Jonse's outbreak. "It is not mutton. This is lamb. Are you going to let an old prejudice judge your food instead of your stomach?"

Jonse grinned sheepishly. "Put that way, maybe you're right."

He cautiously cut off another bite and put it into his mouth, expecting a minor rebellion from his tongue. The old prejudice lost the argument with his tongue. His eyes opened in surprise. "It's good. Damned good."

Jonse smiled in apology at Marita. "I guess I'm hardheaded about some things, Marita."

Her smile said how quickly she accepted the apology and forgave him. "Show me a man that isn't," she said.

Jonse had never eaten a better meal. "That mutton I tried didn't taste like this," he said in final argument.

Marita shook her head. "And they say a woman must have the last word."

Jonse grinned at Luis's burst of enjoyment. "I told you, you cannot win against her," Luis said.

"It looks like you're right," Jonse admitted.

Jonse finished his meal and leaned back. "I apologize for not having shaved," he said. "When I looked at myself in a mirror, I saw what a tough time I'd have getting a razor through these scabs." Right now, he looked like a godawful mess. Maybe Marita was right when she said those scratches would heal without leaving permanent evidence of his encounter with the lion. He was lucky, he reflected soberly. It was a small wonder that the cat hadn't ripped his face wide open.

Jonse was barefoot, knowing that the tussle of pulling on his boots would cost him more than the effort was worth. His pants had been washed and mended. The cat had put a few rips in them too, but they were serviceable. The shirt was a hopeless ruin. Not even the most skillful seamstress could do much about repairing it. Marita had enlarged one of Luis's shirts, a white, formless garment. Even after letting out the seams, it was still uncomfortably tight.

Jonse shifted in his chair and grimaced.

"You hurt," Marita said instantly.

"Some," he admitted. "But it's better than when I first came to last night." He shook his head in sober memory.

Luis's eyes glowed. "It must have been a memorable fight."

Jonse shook his head. "Not for me. I'd like to forget it as soon as possible."

Luis ignored the warning in Marita's shaking head. "I want to hear about it," he said stubbornly.

Jonse stared blankly across the room. "Couldn't have lasted more than a couple of minutes in all. My God, I thought it would go on forever. I heard that cat scream and knew I should move Cribber closer to the camp. He was hobbled." Jonse seemed completely unaware that anybody else was in the room with him. The scene rushed back at him, and he relived it all over again. "The cat sprang at Cribber before I could reach him. Cribber reared and knocked him to the ground. But Cribber got in my way, and I couldn't get a clear shot at the cat. Just when I thought I might get a shot, Streak rushed by me and tangled with the lion. They were so tangled together I couldn't get a shot at all. The only thing I could think of was to try and knock the cat off Streak with the butt of my rifle. I got in a lucky blow across the cat's nose. It hurt him enough to make him forget all about Streak, and he broke free of him. I lost my rifle and grabbed my pistol just before he leaped on me. After that about all I remember is I just kept pulling the trigger."

"*Dios*," Luis breathed. "I have never heard of such bravery."

Jonse shook his head. "It wasn't bravery," he said flatly. "I was just plain scared. My concern was for Streak and Cribber," he conceded, "but I had enough room left for plenty of fear just for me."

Luis waggled a forefinger back and forth, denying what Jonse said. Jonse thought Luis must be around twenty years old, and he was insistent upon making a hero out of Jonse. It was flattering, but it wasn't really true.

"The thing that is truly amazing is that you got the three of us back here," Jonse said.

Luis shrugged, modestly disclaiming that any particular praise should go to him, though he would not look directly at Jonse. "It was *nada*," he muttered. "I got you on my horse and hurried to bring you here. It was not far. Maybe two miles, a little more."

Jonse stared at Luis in amazement, trying to visualize how this small man could lift him. That slight figure certainly didn't seem capable of it.

"I don't see how you did it," Jonse said in flat denial.

Luis ducked his head. "I can tell you it was a struggle. Fortunately, Ramon is an old and tired horse. He learned long ago that he will only wind up by obeying. Now he obeys at once and gets it over with. The smell of the blood did make him a little nervous, but he knew better than to arouse me." He chuckled at some memory. "Madre was the one who was scared when she saw you. She helped me get you inside. Then I had to return for your dog and horse. They were not difficult."

Luis told his story with no embellishment as though what he had done was no more than a trip to town to pick up a sack of flour.

"I don't know how to thank you," Jonse said solemnly.

"Ho," Luis jeered. "What I did was *nada*. All your thanks should go to Marita. During all those days and nights, if she slept, I did not know of it. No matter what hour of the night it was, I found her bending over you, changing a bandage, or putting some salve on your wounds. I could tell by her face how you were doing. Until last night, I had every doubt, then when she came out, her face was shining. She looked like an angel."

"Stop it, Luis," Marita said in quick embarrassment. "You make me sound like a—a—" She hesitated as she couldn't find the word she wanted.

"An angel?" Jonse suggested. He grinned with delight at the blush that covered Marita's face. "You were that to me. And more." He looked gravely from face to face. He owed these two more than he could ever possibly repay. At least, they were entitled to know why he was here in the first place.

"My wife was murdered a little over a month ago." He kept his tone emotionless, and that was a minor accomplishment. He related the entire matter in the same flat words. "My wife told me what her attacker looked like before she died."

"She meant much to you," Marita said softly as Jonse paused.

"Much" was an understatement, but Jonse did not correct her. "Yes," he said simply. "Ever since, I have been looking for her killer. I chased him out of Texas and into New Mexico. Several times, I was sure I had lost him, then I found somebody who remembered a redheaded man with a scarred face who passed through. I was getting close to him. I was only a day at the most behind him when the mountain lion stopped me. But I'll find him. It'll only take me a little longer." He looked from Marita to Luis. "Did either of you see such a man?"

Both gravely considered his question, then shook their heads. "But that is not surprising," Marita hastened to say. "This is an out-of-the-way place. Rarely do we see anybody." She chewed at her lower lip before she asked, "You are determined to keep on?"

Jonse's anger flared at Marita's question. That was a damn-fool thing to ask. Of course he was going on; there was no other route left open to him. His anger grew, and he snapped, "Do you expect me to forgive him?"

"No," Marita said, shaking her head. "I understand your hating. But it is such a bad thing. When hate possesses one, it devours him completely."

Jonse made an angry gesture, stopping whatever else she might want to say. He owed her a lot, but he didn't want to sit here and listen to a lecutre.

"I'm leaving in the morning," he said grimly. "I can make it."

"But how?" Marita cried. "I heard Luis tell you your horse is recovering, but that does not mean he is ready to travel. Do you want to break open his wound? The dog is a long way from being able to accompany you."

Jonse scowled at her. Nothing angered one more than to be faced with cold facts, particularly when those facts were the opposite of what one wanted to do.

"I was going to ask you to take care of Streak until I could return." Jonse realized he was asking for more favors, but this time he was helpless to avoid it. "I'd like to leave Cribber too. Luis, couldn't I take one of your horses?"

"It would be the only one," Luis replied. "Amigo, you are welcome to him, but as I told you, he is very old and tired. He could not carry you far."

Jonse felt as though he were being hemmed in, and he wanted to yell his protest. "I've got a little money with me. I can buy a horse from one of your neighbors."

An odd exchange of glances flashed between Marita and Luis. "We have only one neighbor." Marita's voice was barely audible. "A neighbor so big that all the land around us belongs to one family. That family does not look with pleasure at us. They would do no favor for us, however hard we might beg."

Jonse groaned inwardly. He had landed in the middle of some kind of a feud. Oh damn it! Everything seemed to be working against him. He looked at the two pairs of brown eyes that studied him intently. Did he imagine those eyes had a fearful apprehension in them as they awaited his reaction? His momentary anger against them had been childish, and he apologized mentally to both of them. If it hadn't been for them, he wouldn't be here at all.

He managed a stiff smile. "Then I guess I haven't much to say about it, do I?"

That was relief on Marita's face as she leaned toward Jonse. "I am glad," she said. "In the long run, it will work out for the best. You will see."

It was hard to keep from yelling at her. How could this work out for the best when every passing day was throwing him farther behind the redheaded one?

Jonse had the odd feeling Luis wanted to say something that might clear up the mystery of Higueras' situation, but Luis had closed his mouth without saying a word. Had Jonse caught a barely perceptible shake of Marita's head at her son, or was that more imagination?

One thing was certain. The high spirits of a few moments ago were gone. Luis looked soberly at the table, and Jonse was sure the strain around Marita's mouth had returned.

Should he bluntly ask them what trouble they were in, or would that be too much like prying? He decided against personal questions. If they wanted him to know, they would tell him.

Jonse sat there a half hour longer, then excused himself. "I got tired quicker than I expected," he explained.

"I should look at the wounds again," Marita exclaimed.

Jonse shook his head. "They're getting along just fine. I'll see both of you in the morning."

He closed the bedroom door behind him. He wished he could hear the conversation between them after he left. That would explain a lot of things. He angrily shook his head. He had no right to pry.

Jonse made two turns around the small room, forcing his legs to the utmost. The exertion brought out a thin film of sweat on his forehead, and the pain was returning. Marita was a wise woman. She was right when she said he was unable to travel yet.

He sank into bed, breathing hard, and scowled at the ceiling. Everywhere he turned, he faced a blank wall, and there seemed to be no way to get through it.

CHAPTER SIX

JONSE DIDN'T SLEEP well that night. It wasn't the pain of his wounds that kept him awake, though he was a long way from being able to completely forget them. No, his troubled thoughts kept sleep from him. He worried over his own problem, and he thought soberly about the Higueras' problem. He didn't know what that problem was, but he knew they had one.

He slept fitfully until the crowing of a rooster awakened him. He didn't have to see the sun to know how early it was. The rooster crowed again, and Jonse growled at him. "If you were mine, you'd wind up in the pot."

He went back to the perplexities that seemed to have him hemmed in. He couldn't stay here much longer, presuming on the Higuera hospitality, but under present conditions he couldn't very well leave, either. He fell into a troubled sleep, trying to pick his way clear of all the things that pressured him.

Jonse didn't know how much later it was when his eyes flew open with a start. Was that part of another dream, or had he actually heard the rumble of wheels? He lay there, thinking about the difference in the sound of wheels. A heavy wagon's wheels had a far different sound, with a ponderous rolling that had an earthshaking quality. This sound Jonse thought he heard was a lighter sound, a light whirring of noise that suggested speed.

"Gasper," an imperious voice said. "I will be gone only a few minutes."

Jonse was fully awake now. That voice was coming from the outside of the house.

"Si, Señora Higuera," Gasper replied. His voice reeked of deference. It suggested that Gasper would never dare cross this woman.

Jonse frowned. That was not Marita's voice, though the last name was the same. Probably some relative paying Marita a visit, though it seemed unusually early for a visit.

Jonse climbed out of bed and crossed to the window, curious enough to want a glimpse of this woman.

She came toward the house, her head carried regally. Her face was as frozen as that of a statue, the cheekbones standing out starkly on the white cheeks. Every line of her face radiated a cold, controlled fury.

Jonse whistled softly. He could say with a degree of certainty that this woman sought no pleasure in this visit. He couldn't say about Marita, for he couldn't see her, but how could she possibly react without hostility toward the fury that was in this woman?

The last name was the same, but that was no indication of anything. In the brief appraisal of the woman Jonse had seen no family resemblance in this woman to Marita. Jonse had the feeling the visitor had never known a giving moment in her life. She reeked of haughtiness and contempt, and Jonse would put her down as the kind who crushed people, not helped them.

Jonse grimaced. He was making one hell of a judgment from only a brief appraisal. One thing he could be sure of, this woman came from the wealthy class. Her clothes were evidence of affluence. A rich relative visiting a poor one, Jonse decided. Distaste was plain in the woman's face. Jonse could bet this visit would be as short as possible.

The woman passed out of Jonse's view, and he looked at the carriage. If the woman's clothes hadn't screamed wealth, the carriage did. Jonse had never seen a more beautiful one. A poor family could live for a long time on what this vehicle cost.

Gasper was a further indication of that wealth, for he was in elegant livery. He sat stiffly on the box, looking straight ahead. Jonse would say the man didn't dare draw a free breath while his mistress was close by.

"Why are you here?" That was Marita's voice, the anger in it, raising it above its normal volume.

Jonse's eyebrows arched. The tone erased any doubt he might have of any good feeling between the two.

"I do not intrude on you," Marita went on in that cold, remote voice. "I demand the same courtesy from you."

Jonse whistled soundlessly. Marita couldn't put it any straighter than that. He wondered if Luis was with Marita; if he wasn't, did Marita need help? Jonse remembered that tough spiritual quality in Marita. She wouldn't need any help against another woman.

Marita spoke up again, relieving Jonse of any wonder of where Luis was. "Luis, you keep silent. This is none of your affair. I can do whatever is necessary."

"You can do nothing," the other woman sneered. "Only as much as I want you to."

Jonse's eyebrows rose again. He couldn't see the two women, but it sounded like they faced each other like a pair of spitting, enraged cats.

"Do you know what day this is?" the visitor demanded.

"How could I ever forget?"

Jonse almost missed those words. Marita's voice was much lower.

"It was six months ago to the day that Bernal died." The woman's voice rose with each word until she was almost shouting.

Jonse winced at the vehemence in the voice, wondering if this brought particular distress to Marita. The woman was gloating over the fact she was the one to deliver the news.

Marita's voice strengthened, and her contempt was naked. "Do you think you have to remind me of that? I would remember far better than you."

Jonse frowned. He hadn't the slightest idea of what this was all about, but he had never heard such open animosity in two voices. He wondered if he should go in and break this up, then rejected the impulse. Marita's son was with her; he could do anything that was necessary to protect Marita. Besides, this was no business of Jonse's, and interfering could possibly make the two women turn on him.

He moved closer to the door. If this disagreement grew more heated, somebody might have to do something to break it up.

"I thought by now you would have the decency to leave, after all the harm you have done," the woman hissed. "All these years you have done your best to destroy a family. Yet, you insist upon squatting here, hoping to do more harm."

"I am not a squatter," Marita said firmly. "This is my house, my land." Triumph was undisguised in her voice. "There is nothing you can do to change that."

A long silence followed, and Jonse could imagine the strange woman sucking in her enraged breath.

"I will make you a final offer," Señora Higuera finally said. "You will take it, or—"

Marita interrupted her. "Is it more than you offered before?" Marita taunted. "Then it will be less than the land's actual value. If you offered ten times more, the answer would still be no."

Jonse waited tensely. He could imagine Señora Higuera's face going white, while she struggled for breath. If there was ever a moment for violence, this was it.

"You will regret your foolishness," the woman said in a low, deadly voice. "I promise you will be driven out with nothing. Do not smirk at me," she raged. "I have ways."

"Then use them," Marita said with forced calmness. "But for now, you will get out of my house."

Jonse heard the hard thrust of feminine heels driven against the floor, then the front door slammed.

He moved to the window and watched the woman climb into her carriage. "Why are you sitting there, Gasper?" the woman yelled. "Go!"

Jonse's face was thoughtful as he watched the coachman whip the matched team of bays into action. Jonse did not know who the woman was, or the basis for the quarrel, but he knew it was based on something of long standing. He would not discount anything the señora said. Marita didn't sound as though she were afraid of her, but Jonse would advise Marita to avoid her as she would a poisonous snake.

Jonse dressed slowly, giving the people in the other room time to compose themselves. He couldn't say anything about what he had heard unless they invited him into the discussion. Remembering the resolute cut of Marita's chin, he doubted that would be likely.

He tugged on his boots, grimacing at the effort it took. He was still a long way from being back to normal, but he could get around, if he took it slowly.

Jonse walked into the kitchen where Luis sat at the table, his face despondent, his eyes unseeing. What Luis had witnessed and heard had shaken him badly.

Jonse looked around the room. "Marita not here?" he asked in pretended surprise. After a quarrel as intense as this one, he could believe that tears would be Marita's only relief.

The strain was back in Luis's face as he lifted his head and looked at Jonse. "She is in her room. She has not yet finished dressing." He told the lie badly. Luis sighed, then said, "Breakfast will be ready soon.

"Good," Jonse responded. "That will give us time

to go out and see Cribber and Streak.''

Instant alarm flashed across Luis's face. ''Do you think you should go out so soon? I am not sure Marita would approve—'' He let the remainder trail away as he shook his head.

Marita might disapprove, Jonse thought, if she knew about him going out. But she had far graver problems on her mind than him.

Jonse walked outside. Luis watched each step he took. ''Is it bad, yes?'' he asked sympathetically.

''I'm not ready to run a race right now,'' Jonse grunted. ''But I'll get by.'' Each step brought an accompanying twinge of pain. How right Marita was when she said he was in no shape to even be thinking of traveling now. But he was moving far better than he had last night.

Luis walked over to a woodpile, picked through it, and came back with a stick some three feet in length. At the negative look on Jonse's face, he said, ''Use it, amigo. There are times when a man needs a third leg.''

''I didn't think I'd come to this so soon,'' Jonse replied. But Luis was right. It did ease his walking tremendously. His face sobered at a depressing thought. How long would it take to catch up with the redheaded man at this rate? He would not live that long, he thought in quick misery.

As he walked Jonse looked about the place. It was neat and clean, showing the effort of a constant struggle. The adobe house was small, but it had been recently whitewashed, and its whiteness glistened in the weak fall sun. The few outbuildings showed the same care. While this place didn't have a threadbare look of poverty about it, it certainly showed struggle. Marita and Luis were making a living but not a whole lot more.

Jonse kept glancing at Luis, waiting for him to say something about the quarrel, but Luis kept his lips clamped tight. The expression prevented Jonse from intruding as firmly as a stoutly locked door.

Streak must have heard Jonse coming, for he barked frantically. The bark had vigor, and the sound lifted Jonse's heart. The barking came from the shed. Streak sensed Jonse was out here, but why didn't he come bounding out of the shed toward him as he always did?

Luis caught the worry in Jonse's eyes and said, "An animal is smarter than a man. He is content to let nature heal him. He will not push himself beyond the limits of his present capabilities."

Jonse couldn't argue with that, but why wasn't Streak coming? Then he saw him coming through the shed door, hobbling so painfully. One paw was lifted from the ground as he moved. That put a new concern in Jonse. Evidently, Streak had been unable to use that injured paw since the night of his entanglement with the cat. Jonse had seen other dogs who had been as critically hurt and never used the paw again, even when the injury was completely healed. Once a dog was convinced he was badly hurt, he did not try the foot again. Jonse felt a tightening in his throat. He did not want that happening to Streak.

Jonse dropped to his knees, holding out his arms. "Here boy," he called. "Come on."

Jonse's voice and the sight of him sent Streak into an ecstasy of delight. He limped forward, forgetting about carrying the injured paw. His former dash was sadly missing, but he was moving on all fours.

Streak leaped on him, and Jonse hugged him hard, disregarding the twinges of pain Streak's wriggling provoked in him. He licked Jonse's face over and over, trying to tell Jonse how happy he was to see him.

Streak was making a mess of Jonse's shirt. The dog was literally smeared with grease, and each wriggle put a new stain on Jonse's shirt.

"Damn it, Streak," Jonse complained. "Stop it." He looked up at Luis. "Look what he's doing to me."

"I smeared him with grease," Luis said as he grinned. "I thought it would keep infection down. And it keeps away the stinging of the flies." He shrugged such an unimportant matter away. "Do not worry about it. Marita will launder it for you, or she will make you a new one."

Jonse finally got Streak calmed down so he could examine him more closely. The dog's wounds were healing, but Jonse could see the scratches that crisscrossed his body. Some of them were deep. They told of what an appalling amount of punishment he had taken.

Jonse put a final pat on Streak's head and got to his feet, grunting with the effort it took. Luis picked up Jonse's stick and handed it to him.

"We almost bit off more than we could chew, didn't we, boy?" Jonse asked. Now, he could believe that Streak would recover completely. He wanted to see Cribber.

He limped into the shed, Streak never leaving his heels. Cribber looked as good as Jonse had ever seen him. He was fat and sassy; Cribber had been eating well.

Jonse couldn't see a mark on the gelding, and he looked questioningly at Luis.

"On the other side," Luis said softly.

Jonse limped around Cribber. He sucked in his breath as he saw the ghastly scar. It started at the withers and ran half the length of the foreleg. Jonse shuddered as he thought of those claws biting a little deeper. He was fortunate to have either of these animals alive.

He examined the wound without touching it. It had scabbed over, and he saw no trace of infection. In another week or so, the scab would drop away, but the scar would always remain.

"You're one hell of an animal doctor," Jonse said gruffly.

Luis shrugged away the compliment, but his eyes were pleased. "Both of them are tough," he said. "That made it easlier."

Jonse nodded and walked outside, his face thoughtful. Marita was right when she said he could not possibly leave now. Neither he, nor Cribber, were in any shape to contemplate a trip of any distance, and it was absolutely out of the question for Streak. The rebellion inside him screamed at the thought of all that lost time, and there could readily be much more. A saner thought counseled him, Forget about the redhead. You cannot catch up with him now.

Jonse closed his mind to such thoughts. Arguing against them now would solve nothing. All he could do was wait as placidly as he could.

Jonse forced himself back to reality. "Taking care of them doubled your work load, didn't it?" he asked Luis.

Luis shrugged again. "It wasn't that bad," he disclaimed. "I had help."

Jonse walked over to the woodpile and sat down. Sure, Luis and Marita. Jonse knew what she had endured.

"I don't see how you two managed it all," Jonse said. "There's your own living to think about."

Streak sat down at Jonse's feet. Those scabs must be itching, for Streak dug vigorously at them. Streak might reopen some of those scratches, but Jonse could see no effective way of keeping him from doing that.

"In some way, I will repay you two," Jonse said gravely. He was aware there had been a new irritability in Luis all morning. What he said seemed to add fuel to that irritabilty, for Luis flared. "I have told you it is *nada*," he shouted. He calmed himself, and his voice lowered. "Marita and I were not alone. Old Pancho helped me. He is my sheepherder. He was around when I needed more help."

For a moment, Jonse thought Luis was going to pour out a torrent of words, but the words never came. Instead, Luis shrugged. A shrug seemed to be his favorite answer to every perplexing problem. "We managed."

Jonse studied him. He felt sure Luis was on the verge of pouring out whatever troubled him. "Maybe it would do some good to talk about it," Jonse said gently. "When one can't see the way out of a hole, sometimes another head can help."

"You cannot help me," Luis said, a sulky note in his voice. "Nobody can." He was silent a moment, then burst out, "Why is such a rocky road laid out for one, and another never sees a stone? There is no help for such as me. I am a bastard."

Jonse grinned to himself. Luis was really in a self-recriminatory mood this morning. "At one time or another, every man can call himself that, Luis. I've known several times when that description fit me pretty good."

The levity didn't touch Luis at all. He stared stonily ahead. "You do not understand at all," he muttered. "I am an actual bastard. The world does not have a place for such a one."

Jonse's eyes narrowed. Luis meant the literal meaning of the word "bastard." Jonse didn't know what kind of a hole Luis was in, but from what he said, it wasn't all his digging. Maybe he would never know a better time to reach out a helping hand to Luis.

"Luis," he said sharply. "Does all this have something to do with Bernal?"

Luis's eyes showed his shock. "You heard this morning before you came out of your room?"

Jonse nodded. "I also saw the woman your mother called Señora Higuera. I didn't want to listen, Luis, but I couldn't help it. Their voices were pretty loud.

I have never heard so much hating as in Señor Higuera's voice."

Luis seemed to collapse inwardly. He groaned and whispered, "You wouldn't believe so much hate. That woman would like nothing better than to see my mother dead. Yes, and me, too."

Luis was living in an agony of self-torment, and Jonse waited for him to go on. This could be what Jonse was looking for; this could be the way to repay Marita and Luis for everything they had done for him.

Jonse's voice hardened. "I think you'd better tell me about it, Luis."

Luis shook his head in dogged refusal. "I cannot," he cried. "It is not up to me."

Jonse wanted to grab Luis and shake the stubbornness out of him. He was searching for better words to make Luis see reason; then Luis muttered, "If Marita wants to talk to you about it, I would not stop her. This is solely her affair."

"Good," Jonse said briskly and struggled to his feet.

Luis handed Jonse his walking stick.

"Don't know how I'd get along without that," Jonse said and grinned.

Luis didn't respond to the grin.

CHAPTER SEVEN

JONSE STOPPED STREAK at the door of the house. "You can't come in, boy," he said as he patted Streak's head. "You go back to the shed with Cribber. I'll see you soon."

Streak looked at Jonse and whined dolefully. He decided Jonse meant what he said, for he turned and limped back toward the shed. It really hurt to see Streak hobbling about like this.

Marita had breakfast almost ready when Jonse and Luis entered the house. The smell of food reminded Jonse how hungry he was.

Marita tried to flash him a smile, but it was a miserable failure. She ducked her head, but not in time to prevent Jonse from seeing her red, swollen eyes. She had been crying hard. This morning had been hell for Marita and her son.

"Marita, look what Streak did to my shirt. He got grease all over it."

Marita gave Jonse a quick, little sideways glance before she jerked her eyes away. "It does not matter," she said listlessly.

She placed a platter of fried mush on the table. "That is all I have this morning," she apologized. She went to the stove and came back with the coffee pot and a bottle of syrup.

"Fried mush and syrup," Jonse said heartily. "Who would want a better breakfast than that?"

Luis and his mother ate with poor appetites. Marita took only a couple of bites, and Jonse noticed her hand trembled each time she raised her fork to her mouth.

"Luis," she said. "We are out of everything."

There was a despair in her voice, and Jonse caught the fright in the look they exchanged.

Jonse laid down his fork and looked at Marita. He was as tense as though he were getting ready to jump into ice-cold water, but he could see no better time to clear the air.

"Who is Bernal, Marita?" he asked quietly.

Marita gasped, and her face turned alternately white and red. "You heard her this morning," she exclaimed.

"I couldn't help it," Jonse replied. He would make no other explanation or apology.

Marita's head rose defiantly, and for a moment Jonse feared she was going to flay him for prying into her private business.

Then she buried her face in her hands, and her voice was barely audible. "Bernal was my husband. He died six months ago from a fall off a horse." Her voice rose in a thin wail. "I could not see him before he died, nor attend his funeral."

Jonse frowned. Marita was terribly wrought up. Her explanation was making no sense at all.

"I am a wicked woman," Marita whispered. "The

good *Dios* will never forgive me. Bernal was my husband, but I was not legally married to him."

That made Jonse suck in a hard breath. He looked covertly at Luis. Luis's face was frozen in agony as he stared straight ahead. But Luis Higuera was all wrong. A bastard didn't know who his father was. Luis knew. Jonse felt a rushing pity for the two of them. Good Lord, the self-imposed burden these two were carrying. God wouldn't punish either of them, but how people would.

"It happens that way sometimes," Jonse said thoughtfully. "But I don't see any reason for you to flog yourselves over it." He heard Marita's broken sob, reached out, and pulled her hands from her face.

"I think it's time to talk about it," he said gently.

Marita's eyes brimmed with tears, but she didn't look away from him. "I could not help myself." She overcame the catch in her voice and went on, "It started so many years ago. Twenty-one to be exact."

Jonse nodded. His guess at Luis's age was right. Why hadn't Bernal married Marita? Then the obvious answer hit him. Bernal was already a married man.

"Ah," he said softly. "Bernal was married to the woman who was here this morning."

Marita nodded mutely, as her eyes begged Jonse for understanding. "Though we were not married, Bernal insisted I use his name. He said we could never be more married, if a thousand priests said words over us." She gulped hard to enable herself to go on. "There was never any love between Bernal and Eulalia. The marriage was arranged by Bernal's and Eulalia's families when they were quite young. Bernal could not go against his father's wishes."

Jonse grimaced. He had heard of such arrangements before, where it was more important to satisfy the families than the participants in the actual marriage. He couldn't find it in his heart to censure Bernal or Marita; the blame lay on the families involved for condemning their offspring to a marriage that could be worse than slavery.

"Bernal couldn't do anything about his marriage," Jonse guessed, "because of his religion."

"Mine too," Marita whispered. "Divorce would be worse than what we did. Bernal would have been committed to eternal perdition."

Jonse nodded, his jaw set. He understood too well how a minister or a priest could put terrible chains about a person, rendering them completely helpless. He had known a couple of ministers who swore to bring down the wrath of God upon somebody who displeased the ministers by crossing them, either openly or subtly. He could well imagine how Marita's church must have thundered and roared.

"Marita," he commanded. "Look at me! Did you bring happiness to Bernal? Were you happy with him?"

She closed her eyes briefly in memory. "Two people could never be happier. I think only his trips over here saved his sanity. Eulalia was a cold, domineering woman. She demanded her way, or she screamed."

Jonse thought of the woman's voice earlier this morning. She was a screamer all right. Being around such a woman could be a living hell for a man.

Jonse knew how Marita felt about Bernal. Now, he wanted to hear from Luis.

"Luis, did you like your father?" he asked softly.

Luis's eyes shone. "I only lived until I could see him again. He gave us everything we have."

Marita nodded mute confirmation.

"You have committed no sin," Jonse said practically. "Do you think God was displeased because two people made each other happy? Marita, all this time, you have been blaming yourself because other people demanded you should. Bernal would have known no happiness at all, if it hadn't been for you. Instead of praying for forgiveness, just thank God for the opportunity you had to let Bernal know a little happiness."

Marita's eyes widened as she stared at Jonse. "Do you think it could be so?" she asked fearfully.

Jonse smiled at her. "I know it." His tone was positive. He turned his head toward Luis. "And you just be proud that you had such a father. You keep your head high."

Jonse was pleased at the change in their faces. But one thing worried him, and he wanted to straighten it out.

"That woman said something about driving you out. Can she do it?"

A fierce light appeared in Marita's eyes. "This is my land. Bernal gave it to me."

Jonse's heart sank. Marita knew this was her land, for Bernal had given it to her. But Bernal's intentions and legal proof of ownership were two far different things.

"How much land did he give you?"

"Three thousand acres," Marita answered. "He said it was the finest grazing land he owned."

Jonse whistled. That was a sizable chunk of land. No wonder Bernal's wife was so enraged. "Did he just tell you he was giving you this land, or did he give you proof of your ownership?''

"He gave me a deed," Marita said proudly. "He insisted that I have it recorded. She cannot touch it."

Jonse blew out a relieved breath. That lifted a load off his shoulders. "Bernal must have owned a lot of land to give away so much."

"So much that even Bernal never knew exactly how much land he owned," Marita said in a breathless voice. "It was originally a grant given by the king of Spain. Bernal said it reached from mountain range to mountain range, from river to river. His grandfather left it to his son, and Bernal's father left it to Bernal."

"You'd think Señora Higuera would be content with what she has left," Jonse said thoughtfully.

"She cannot stand that I am living near her," Marita said passionately. "She has made offers to buy this land before. I think this morning's offer will be her last one. Hah," she said scornfully. "She should know by now I will never sell."

Jonse's eyes narrowed. Marita must never make the mistake of underestimating Señora Higuera. The Señora was obviously a powerful, influential woman, and with the hatred built up over the years, she could be deadly.

"Does she hire many *vaqueros*?" Jonse asked.

"Many," Luis replied.

Jonse pulled at an earlobe. "I don't see why she hasn't just ridden over you two by now."

Marita shook her head slowly as though she too wondered about that. She shrugged and said, "Perhaps she does not dare go that far. She could be afraid to turn the country against her."

Jonse's eyebrows raised skeptically. From what he had put together, he would say Señora Higuera considered herself a scorned woman, and it was driving her wild.

"Has she actually bothered you?" he asked.

Luis spoke up. "Yes, in many little ways. They run cattle, vast herds of them. Her sons have promised me that one of these days, they would drive their cattle onto our land, and leave nothing for our sheep to eat. Two men I hired as sheepherders disappeared. Whether they were frightened off or bought off, I do not know. If Pancho should leave us, I doubt we could find another willing to work for us." Luis's face was troubled. "That is why we have only five hundred sheep. I am afraid we could not handle more. Even so, some of our sheep disappear from time to time. I do not dare wander about on her land, looking for them. Her sons have told me what would happen, if I did."

Jonse groaned inwardly. This was the first he had heard of sons. "How many sons?" he asked.

"Three," Luis answered.

Three sons, Jonse thought bleakly, with exactly the same feelings toward Marita as their mother. That could only be expected. Jonse had never seen a more thoroughly complicated mess. Plus the hatred engendered by normal human passions, there was the age-old dislike between cattlemen and sheepmen.

Marita looked at Jonse's hard, reflective face. "Do not worry about us. She has ridden over here before to threaten us. Nothing happened. Nothing will."

She seemed confident, Jonse thought, too entirely confident, and he suspected her words were said to relieve him. Marita Higuera had pride, she would not want to pull him into a problem that she felt was entirely hers.

Jonse had listened to a furious woman this morning and caught a glimpse of an enraged face. If he had to pick out an enemy, it would always be a man. A woman was too hard to fight, for she could hit you in so many unsuspected, devious ways. Señora Higuera's passions had mounted month after month until now they were boiling over, and in that spilling, Marita and Luis were bound to be hurt.

He looked at Luis. "You said something about needing supplies?"

Luis nodded, his face tight at the memory. "I rode into town three days ago. I could not buy supplies anyplace. Every store was out of everything I asked for."

"But you didn't think they were out?" Jonse asked.

"I know they were not," Luis said violently. "I could see the items I asked for on the shelves." Just the thought of his rejection was turning his face dark.

"Ah," Jonse said speculatively. "This has happened before?"

"Never so bad as this," Luis said. "I could buy nothing."

"Why does the entire town side in with Señora Higuera?"

Luis's short burst of laughter had a bitter ring. "It is a very small town with only a few stores. It is built on land my father owned. He started the town many years ago, thinking this part of the country needed one."

"Did he give the land to the store owners?" Jonse asked.

Luis shrugged. "I do not know."

Probably Bernal hadn't given away, or deeded any of the stores sites. If so, every store owner was there on Higuera sufferance, and they would gladly obey any suggestion Señora Higuera made. Jonse thought the woman was beginning to tighten the screws on Marita and Luis. This was one of the more devious ways, to be used until it served to drive Marita and Luis out. If it failed, there was always brute force left as a last resort.

Marita looked at Jonse's intent face. "You cannot involve yourself in our troubles. Eulalia would turn as viciously on you as she has turned against us."

Jonse smiled at her. "Might be interesting to find out."

Marita's face was pale as she shook her head. "The one doctor we have in town would not even come out to tend you. Luis asked him and was turned down."

Jonse nodded his understanding. "That means I have only you two to be grateful to. It makes it pretty plain where I should stand, doesn't it?"

"But you will forget about the man you hunt for?" Marita cried.

The answer to that wrenched Jonse. His search would have to be forgotten, for a while anyway. Marcia, you understand, don't you? he begged silently. Maybe this meant he would never find the man he wanted, but Jonse thought he would never feel any guilt about his decision.

Marita's eyes were filling with tears again, and Jonse said briskly, "Here now. I think I'll ride into town and buy a few supplies that we will need. The stores would sell to a stranger, wouldn't they?"

Hope was replacing the blackness on Luis's face. "Yes," he said. "I see no reason why not."

"Can I use Ramon?" Jonse asked. "Cribber is—"

Luis didn't give him time to finish. "You know that without asking," he said fiercely.

Marita was crying openly, her hands to her face.

"Hey," Jonse said plaintively. "My breakfast is getting cold.

CHAPTER EIGHT

RED SCURLOCK LEANED AGAINST the makeshift bar of the cantina, his face set in a heavy scowl. He was a tall man, lean to the point of emaciation. His hair was the obvious reason for his nickname. A ghastly scar bisected his cheek from eye to lip corner. The wound had healed poorly, leaving a twisted, purplish scar. He had tried disguishing it by growing a beard, but even the most luxuriant growth couldn't cover more than half of the scar. He didn't like Mexicans, man or woman, for a Mexican woman had given him that scar.

Scurlock's eyes were smoky as he remembered that incident. The woman had rushed at him when he announced he was leaving for good. He had been careless, thinking she was intent only on clawing him, and he could handle that easily. Until the last split second, he hadn't been aware of the small knife concealed in one of her hands. He caught one wrist and was whirling her around when the other hand slashed at him. The knife blade laid his cheek wide open. He fell back, his face contorted with the sudden rush of pain. A bullet would leave a man numb with shock before the pain flooded in, but a knife was different, for the pain came instantly.

Pressing a hand to the throbbing pain, he stared in dismay at the blood covering his hand, before he could marshal his scattered senses. Then with a roar, he had sprung on the woman, knocking the knife away before she could slash him again.

He had beaten her with heavy blows in a senseless display of unbridled fury. The blows continued long after she ceased whimpering.

Scurlock felt no remorse as he looked at the battered, motionless figure. The goddamned bitch had earned that. He never glanced at her again as he poured water into a wash pan and bathed his wound. For a long while, the pain kept him from thinking clearly. Uneasiness and worry filled him as he finally got the bleeding stopped. He had better get out of town before the woman's body was discovered. He didn't know how tough the law was in this town, but he better take no chances in finding out how severely this Texas law might frown on killing a woman.

Scurlock had ridden out of town, not knowing a free breath until a full week had passed, until he was certain no one was on his trail, but that Mexican whore had cost him. Scurlock cursed her a dozen times. He didn't dare stay in the country where he was known, for fear someone might connect his disappearance with the woman's death. So he had wandered aimlessly, stopping for an odd job for a week or so, then moving to another place. He detested manual labor, but the lowest, menial tasks were about all a total stranger could get. His growing disgust with the rigors of these jobs, plus the employers' dissatisfaction, combined to drive him on.

Scurlock was like water, always flowing downhill, sinking lower and lower. He was an inveterate gambler when he had the money, and once, long ago, he had lived fairly well off his skill. But that skill and luck seemed to have run out when the woman died. Scurlock didn't know what town he was in when he awakened in a livery stable.

The familiar throbbing in his head told him he was drunk. The taste in his mouth was additional confirmation, and his eyes wouldn't focus.

A prodding boot toe finally broke through his stupor. "Come on," an unsympathetic voice said. "Clear out of here."

Scurlock blinked several times before he recognized the livery stable owner. Indignation washed over him in waves. Who in the hell did this man think he was to kick him around like this?

Scurlock sat up, trying to pull himself together. "I just came to get my horse," he said with what dignity he could muster. He noticed for the first time that his holster was empty, and he said in instant alarm, "I must've lost my gun on the way here."

"You really poured down a load, didn't you? I watched part of that game you were in. Mister, you haven't got a gun, or a horse. You lost both of them."

Scurlock's groan didn't move the stable owner's face to pity. "You should've started thinking this way before you started drinking."

Flashes of last night returned to Scurlock. For a stretch during the game, he thought his luck had returned, and he remembered buying a round of drinks for everybody at the table. As his winnings mounted, he ordered another round, then another. He didn't remember just when his luck left him; after that, he didn't remember much of anything.

The stable owner cackled at the look on Scurlock's face. "I guess you wandered in here because you didn't have any other place to go. When I came back, you were sleeping on this hay pile. I tried to wake you, but it was impossible. I gave up and let you sleep it off until morning. Mister, get out of here. If I need help, I can get the sheriff."

Scurlock's face was twisted and mean as those memories washed over him. "Another shot," he ordered harshly from the fat, swarthy man behind the bar.

"Si, señor," the man agreed amiably and waddled over to pour another drink.

Scurlock almost gagged as he got this rotten liquor down. This poor quality fitted with the rest of this sorry, miserable town.

He couldn't keep his thoughts from going back to the morning when he awakened from his sodden slumber. He had begged the stable owner for a job, anything, even cleaning out the stalls, for his pockets were completely empty.

That hardhearted bastard had ears of stone. He wouldn't even loan Scurlock enough money to buy a drink, and breakfast was completely out of the question. When the stable owner threatened to call the sheriff, Scurlock stumbled out into the street.

He hitched a ride on a freight wagon and sat there half dozing, never really hearing what the driver said. He guessed he had ridden ten or twelve miles when his attention was caught by the small neat white house just off of the road.

"I'll get off here," Scurlock said suddenly.

It surprised the driver, but he hauled up the teams. "Sure this is where you want to go?"

Scurlock managed a strained grin. "One place is as good as another, isn't it?"

"If it suits you, it suits me," the driver replied before he lifted the reins.

Scurlock stood beside the road, watching the wagon disappear around a bend. He didn't know who lived in the little house, but perhaps he could get a small job around the place. At least, he should be able to talk himself into some breakfast.

There was no one in sight as Scurlock approached the house. His repeated calls received no answer. Evidently the occupants were not home. He hesitated briefly, then decided this was a good chance to see if he could find anything of value inside.

There might even be some money stashed somewhere. He had nothing to lose; at least he could surely find some food.

There was nothing in the parlor or kitchen that caught his eye. He stood in the doorway of the bedroom thinking, Nothing much in here, either. The dresser drawers yielded nothing of value, but under the paper in the bottom drawer he found some folded bills. Scurlock remembered his exultation as he counted them. He held fifty-five dollars in his hand. His luck had turned!

A small noise at the door of the room caused Scurlock to turn his head, and his heart sank. A woman stood there, her eyes wide in shock.

She looked at the opened drawers and the money Scurlock held, then she screamed.

The scream broke Scurlock's trance, and he

bounded toward her. That damned screaming had to be stopped. He seized her roughly, but she fought like a wildcat, tearing loose from Scurlock's hands. She reached the door of the kitchen before Scurlock could grab her again. My God! Her screams were loud enough to arouse everybody in the country.

Scurlock clamped one arm around her throat, shutting off her breath. With the other hand, he plunged a knife deep into her chest.

The woman fell limply, and Scurlock stepped back, his eyes wild with terror. His breathing eased as he saw that the woman didn't stir. She was dead all right. He wanted to beat his hands together in futile frustration. He hadn't wanted to kill this woman. Why had she picked this moment to come in here? He was shaking so hard that his teeth chattered. Instinctively, he knew this was far more serious than killing the whore. He knew he'd better get out of here. If he was caught, he knew what would happen to him. Already, he could feel the rasping touch of a rope around his neck.

On a kitchen counter lay a pistol, and he grabbed it up. He felt a little better with his holster filled. At least he wasn't completely helpless.

Scurlock's lungs screamed in agony as he ran, pausing only long enough to give them a little relief. Then, he ran again. Sheer exhaustion forced him to a staggering pace when he saw a saddled horse in a corral. He opened the corral gate and mounted. He sank his heels deep into the horse's flanks and never looked back.

Scurlock started at the hand holding the glass. It was trembling again. Fear was his constant companion as he fled. He had kept the stolen horse going for four solid days and was just beginning to believe he was entirely in the clear, when from the vantage of a high hill he saw a distant horseman. He had to stare for a long time before he could be sure that was a dog following the horseman. Could a dog nose out a mounted man? Scurlock didn't know, but just the possibility was enough to send him into wild flight again. Instinct told him this man was trailing him, and he hadn't begun to put enough distance between them.

That relentless pursuit never slackened for a long period. Scurlock had to stop and think, to realize how long it had been. My God, over a month had passed. He had seen the horseman three more times. Scurlock knew it was the same one, for the dog was always with him. Though he never saw the man's face, once he had been close enough to be terrorized by the bulk of his pursuer.

Scurlock had been tempted to lay an ambush but gave up that idea. Armed with only a pistol, he knew he would stand no chance against the rifle he was positive his pursuer carried.

The days and nights blended into one solid, horror-filled nightmare. He couldn't escape from the horror even in sleep, for the nightmare intensified it. It would seize and jerk him out of deep slumber, and even after he calmed his screaming nerves, his muscles would continue to twitch. Each time he thought he lost the following horseman, he saw the figure again. Scurlock hadn't the slightest idea of who the man was, or his connection with this matter but the dogged determination displayed was shocking. Scurlock knew how close he came to going out of his mind. He and the horse were staggering from near exhaustion. He had to stop to rest, but he knew if he did, that pursuer would catch up with him.

Scurlock had no definite idea of where he was, except that he was somewhere in New Mexico. He had avoided the larger towns, and the country had grown steadily wilder. As sparingly as he bought necessary supplies, his money was running low.

He had ridden into this miserable little Mexican town, reeling in the saddle. Regardless of how desperate his plight was, he had to stop for rest.

For a few *centavos* apiece he hired two Mexican kids to watch the road that led through the town. Both boys were promised a reward if they notified him immediately when an American approached on horseback.

For the first time in a month, his sleep was unbroken. He slept a solid eighteen hours. His heart was in his throat when he awakened and found out how long he had slept. Questioning the two kids restored his confidence. Both swore they had seen no stranger. Jesus, he thought in elation. He had lost the horseman. Scurlock decided to stay here as long as he could. The food was sorry, the accomodations poor, but everything was cheap.

Scurlock now considered the small town a sanctuary. It would be foolish to go on and possibly blunder into his pursuer. Besides, his mind and body reveled in the lack of pressure. He hired his two youthful guards each day, promising them the same reward if they kept their eyes open.

Scurlock scowled at his distorted reflection in the cheap back-bar mirror. He would be content to stay here for a long while, if only he had more money. The money in his pocket was down to a few small bills. Even drinking this cheap liquor was a luxury he couldn't afford. Scurlock never considered another robbery. He had seen no one around this town who looked prosperous enough to rob. Even if he found one, Scurlock dared not risk calling attention to himself.

"Another drink, señor?" the bartender asked timidly.

Scurlock shook his head. He'd better start thinking seriously about his expenses.

"Maybe later, Tomas," he said and smiled.

"As you wish, señor," Tomas responded eagerly. He was anxious to keep his best customer happy. "You like our little town, eh?" He steeled himself for rejection. It was rarely that this redheaded man wanted conversation of any kind.

"It is restful," Scurlock acknowledged. "Never felt so relaxed in my life. How long have I been here now?"

Tomas's face brightened. Ah, the stranger wanted to talk. This was *bueno*. It broke up the monotony of one unchanging day after another. "Ten days," Tomas said. "Maybe more. Maybe less. Who keeps track of the days?"

Scurlock managed to keep the smile on his face. Damn him! Scurlock kept track of the days. In all those ten days, there hadn't been the slightest sign of the horseman. Surely, if he appeared anywhere near this town, his presence would be noticed and talked about. No, Scurlock thought, I've lost him. He wanted to stay here just as long as he could. Only one thing would drive him away, money for living expenses.

Tomas was hungry for talk. "You plan to stay here long, señor?"

"I haven't decided yet. Maybe it depends upon finding a job. Anybody around here who's doing any hiring?"

Tomas considered the question at great length. "The only one I know of who is wealthy enough to hire others is Señora Higuera. She can hire hundreds and never think of the cost."

Scurlock's interest quickened. This Señora Higuera was well worth looking into. If she was as wealthy as Tomas said—and Scurlock doubted that, for he hadn't seen anybody around here who even gave the appearance of being rich—it might be to Scurlock's interest to talk to her. The Señora could give him two chances. If she didn't hire him, perhaps there was some way of getting some of her money. Scurlock's facile mind would work on that problem, after he looked the situation over.

"What does this Señora do?" Scurlock asked carelessly.

"Land, señor." Tomas spread his hands to their full extent to show how vast her holdings were. "How much, I doubt if she even knows. You would not believe the number of cattle she owns."

"I might ask her if she needs a hand," Scurlock said thoughtfully.

Tomas looked doubtful. "I do not know, señor. Señora Higuera is a hard woman. All of us are afraid of her. Why shouldn't we be? She controls our lives. She owns even the land this town sits on. If we displease her, she can make us suffer."

Scurlock grimaced. Tomas made her sound tough. "It won't hurt to talk to her, will it?"

Tomas's doubt hadn't lessened. "I do not know, señor. I just do not know."

"Tell me how to get to her place," Scurlock said impatiently.

CHAPTER NINE

EULALIA HIGUERA LOOKED WITH disfavor upon her three sons. At times, she was even positive she hated them. They reminded her too much of Bernal. Her face twisted at the memory of that name. A million times she had cursed him for making her the laughingstock of the country. She would correct that, though at the moment, she didn't see how. She was only a woman, and she needed help. These three would not listen to her. That wasn't quite true. Oh, they listened to her with downcast eyes, but it was apparent their thoughts were elsewhere. They did nothing about her demands. Wasn't Marita Higuera still sitting on land she had no right to?

Eulalia's lips twisted scornfully. That woman had no right to the name Higuera either, yet she still used it.

Eulalia Higuera was a tall, thin woman, carrying her head regally. Even seated, she gave the appearance of towering over others in the room. Her cheeks were hollow, the cheekbones too sharp. The lips were thin, usually pressed together in a tight line. Her eyes were remote and cold, except when they glittered with passion. Her luxurious mass of black hair was streaked with gray. She cursed those ever-widening streaks each time she looked into a mirror. She was getting old, and the thought drove her frantic. The best years of her life had been given to Bernal Higuera, and he had shamed her. Her face did not change, but a single thought pounded madly in her head. She was not going to die with the shame of Marita Higuera on her soul.

God, how she hated Bernal. From the start, his touch had been repugnant, and after her third son was born, she had locked her bedroom door against him. She thought with malicious satisfaction that none of his frenzied entreaties had ever been able to move her.

"What have you done about getting that woman out?" she demanded coldly of her three sons.

Andras, her oldest son, shrugged. "We have instructed everybody in town to have no more dealings with her. No one will sell her a thing, or perform a necessary service for her. It is only a matter of time until the vine withers. It cannot survive when the roots are cut off."

At times, Andras's resemblance to Bernal startled Eulalia. He was outstandingly handsome, but he didn't have his father's drive. He was indolent, preferring to wait for *mañana* to solve a problem for him. *Mañana* could save him the necessity of further effort.

She barely restrained herself from screaming at him. Andras had argued against her stand too often. With all the land they owned, why should she demand that handful of land Marita and her bastard now occupied?

Eulalia forced herself to speak calmly, though agitation was still in her face, and her bosom heaved. "So the three of you have decided that the only way is to sit and wait, regardless of how slowly your mother dies? It does not matter how much disgrace has been heaped upon her. It does not matter she cannot live again until that disgrace is wiped out."

Her words brought distress to Rafael's face, her middle son. Eulalia didn't know where his swarthiness came from. It certainly wasn't in either side of the family. On top of that, Rafael was short and misshapen. It had brought her a constant satisfaction to know that it hurt Bernal each time he looked at Rafael. How many times had she told herself that Rafael's uncomeliness was punishment to Bernal?

She looked coldly at him. Of the three, Rafael probably loved his parents the most. He would try to do anything he could to bring happiness to his mother.

"Just tell us what you want us to do," Rafael begged.

Eulalia stared at him in outrage. It was a simple thing she asked, yet it had to be pointed out to them. "Just drive her out," she hissed. "Run her stock off. Burn down her house and all other buildings. Leave her nothing. She will be glad enough then to go."

Manuel, her youngest, stared at her aghast. He was only eighteen, and if Eulalia had any deep affection for any of them, it was for him. He was slight of stature and fastidious in manner. It pleasured her to think, He is more like me than the others.

"Madre," he cried. "We cannot move as openly as that. It could turn the whole country against us. The law—"

"What law?" she spit at him, cutting him off. "I am the law here. The people wouldn't dare turn against me. I am their very living."

Andras glanced at his brother. "I know what Manuel is trying to say. You want it done all at once. It cannot be done so baldly. Already, we have driven off and killed some of their sheep. Two herdsmen have been destroyed. Before long, no one will even dare go near Marita and her bastard."

Andras liked the word bastard. He mouthed it as though it tasted good.

Eulalia beat at the arm of her chair with her clenched fist. "You propose more waiting. A nibble at a time instead of a single gulp. I want it over."

Manuel and Rafael didn't reply; they were content to let their older brother speak for them.

Andras shook his head. "You say there is no law but you on your land. That is true now. But New Mexico is no longer under Mexican rule. You could bring in the American law. Do you want that?"

Andras's face was concerned, but Eulalia could see the lie just beneath the surface. Andras was a weakling, content to drift through day after day, hoping that something would happen to lift this odious burden from him.

"No," Eulalia screamed. "It will be done my way. The waiting and the doing of nothing is over. Tomorrow—"

She stopped and frowned at the appearance of a servant at the doorway of the room. Salvio knew better than to interrupt her while she was in conference with her sons.

"What is it?" she demanded sharply.

Salvio wrung his hands, the worry apparent on his face. He was a small, abject figure, scarcely daring to breath in the Señora's presence. Her wrath was a terrible thing, and woe be to the person who crossed her and aroused her anger.

"Señora," he begged. "I did not want to interrupt you, but there is an Americano outside. He says it is urgent that he see you."

"Who is it?" she demanded.

Salvio shook his head. "I have never seen him before. But he speaks with great force."

Eulalia gnawed her lower lip. She detested the Americanos and avoided any possible contact with them. But what Andras said about bringing in the American law still rang in her mind. *Dios*, was it possible that Marita had already asked for American help?

Eulalia swallowed her natural instinct to tell the Americano to go away. Perhaps it would be the course of wisdom to see what he wanted.

"Bring him in," she commanded.

She seared her sons with a furious glance. "We will talk about this later." Her tone said that it was not over, not by a long way.

Her lips curled in contempt as she watched her sons straggle out of the room. *Dios*, was she supposed to consider herself blessed with such weaklings?

CHAPTER TEN

SCURLOCK GUESSED HE HAD RIDDEN a good five miles down the lane from where it turned off the main road. Everything he saw increased his growing impression of great wealth. If he owned just a fifth of all of the grazing cattle he saw, he would no longer have to fret about his future.

"This woman must hire a hell of a lot of help," he muttered. He must have seen a dozen *vaqueros*. Most of them looked up from their work as he passed, a few even waved, but none made a motion to approach or question him. That was a relief. He had been afraid that one of them would dash up and order him off this land.

His eyes popped in awe as he came in view of the hacienda. My God, he had never seen a more magnificent house. The adobe walls were built in a long "U," the two wings enclosing a large courtyard.

Scurlock pulled up and sat for a long moment, looking at the house. The taste of envy was bitter in his mouth. All his life he had railed at the unfairness of a few people having so much and the vast majority having nothing. This was an example of that unfairness.

The house was white, and from this distance, he imagined it was whitewashed adobe brick. The roof was red; he was too far away to determine the material used.

Scurlock swore deep in his throat. This damned house was big enough to house a dozen families. A wide veranda ran across the base of the ''U,'' and some kind of flowering vines climbed each pillar, supporting the veranda.

''I'll be goddamned,'' Scurlock said as he looked at the fountain in the middle of the courtyard. How in the hell did people get so lucky to be able to live like this?

He was filled with resentment as he urged the horse forward. It seemed that with all this wealth, there should be a job for him. But this woman would probably treat him like a dog, turning him away before he could fully express his needs. By God, she wasn't going to get away with it, he vowed. She might not hire him, but she would listen to his request.

He rode up to the hacienda and dismounted, tying the reins around one of the pillars. A man, standing in the doorway, watched him as he swaggered onto the veranda.

''Your boss in?'' Scurlock growled. This was a poor little man, frightened out of his wits at any display of force. Probably one of the flunkies, Scurlock thought.

''She is very busy,'' the man said hesitantly. ''I do not know if she will see you.''

''You tell her I demand to see her,'' Scurlock snapped. By God, all the wealth in the world didn't give this Higuera woman the right to brush him off as though he were some kind of insect.

"I will go and ask if she is free," the little man said and darted into the house.

"You be quick about it," Scurlock called after him.

He walked back and forth, impatiently awaiting the man's return. His rage mounted. She wasn't going to turn him out like some begging dog. What can you do about it? a thought mocked Scurlock. His resolve was weakening. He didn't see a thing he could do.

The little man came back surprisingly soon. "Señora Higuera will see you. This way please." He stepped aside for Scurlock to enter, then led the way.

Scurlock's head swam with the grandeur of the furnishings the little man led him past. He had never seen anything like this in his life.

The man opened a door and said, "Señora, this is the one I spoke to you about."

"Show him in," an imperious voice called.

Scurlock stepped into the room and heard the door close behind him. His eyes swept the room, and he could taste his envy. Lord, a fortune must have been spent in just furnishing this room alone.

His eyes went back to the seated woman. He couldn't remember a pair of male eyes looking as tough as the ones now scrutinizing him. They reminded him of a cat's eyes, completely cold with no feeling. Scurlock recalled he hadn't removed his hat, and he snatched it off his head and turned it over and over in his hands.

The gesture of deference seemed to give the woman more assurance, for her voice literally crackled. "What do you want?"

"Are you Señora Higuera?" Scurlock asked.

The woman's hand slashed through the air. "Who else did you expect to find in here?"

Scurlock gulped visibly. This was one tough lady. It radiated in her tone and from her bearing. She was accustomed to complete dominion of every situation she faced.

Scurlock didn't dare stare too long at her, and he jerked his eyes away. But in just that glimpse he noticed the rings on her hands and the necklace dangling from her throat. Damn, there must be a fortune in those jewels.

"Speak up," the woman snapped. "I have not all day to waste. Why did you demand to see me?"

Her manner increased the unease in Scurlock. He would hate to be married to a woman like this. He would bet her husband asked permission to blow his nose.

Scurlock tried to put an ingratiating smile on his face. "I didn't demand," he said mildly. "I only asked to see you."

Those cold eyes glittered as they swept over him again. "Salvio read your bearing wrong," she said icily. "I will speak to him. Why do you wish to see me?"

Scurlock almost winced at the impact of the question. All his former vows had completely vanished. He had sworn to himself he would not cringe before this woman, and here he was doing it.

"Ma'am, I wanted to ask for a job. I need work bad." He was begging and knew it.

Her mirthless burst of laughter sounded like the breaking of a pane of glass. "You dare come in here just to ask me for a job?"

I'd do anything," he said desperately. "You just name it, and it's done."

She's going to kick me out, Scurlock thought in agony. "Surely, ma'am, you've got something that needs doing." He groaned as that impassive face didn't soften. Nothing he could say was going to change her.

"Sit down," she said suddenly. She raised her voice. "Salvio." Not for a moment did she cease studying Scurlock.

What the hell was she going to do now? Scurlock thought in alarm. But after asking him to sit down, she wouldn't be asking for someone to throw him out; or would she?

"Sí, señora," a voice from the doorway said.

Scurlock turned his head. It was the same man who led him to this room. Scurlock hadn't heard Salvio's approach or the door open. Salvio must move like a mouse. Just this brief contact with Señora Higuera made Scurlock appreciate Salvio's fear of arousing his mistress's ire.

"Bring me wine, Salvio," she ordered.

Scurlock felt the nervous tension ebbing out of him. He didn't know where this was going, but her asking him to sit down and ordering wine was in his favor, wasn't it?

Salvio scurried out and returned faster than Scurlock believed possible. He carried a tray, holding a decanter of wine and two glasses. He set the decanter and glasses before her and hastened out of the room. Scurlock didn't know what reason Salvio had to fear Señora Higuera, but it was in his every action.

Señora Higuera's black eyes probed deep as she poured two glasses of wine. Scurlock felt as though they read every thought in his mind.

She held a glass toward Scurlock, and he got to his feet and crossed the floor to take it from her. He felt so damned clumsy and was relieved to retreat to his chair without spilling the wine. He tasted the wine, trying to keep his shaking hand under control.

"Never tasted better wine, ma'am," he said.

"What is your real name?" she said impatiently. "If you should work for me, do not ever try to lie to me."

"Red Scurlock, ma'am," he replied. He felt as though sweat was breaking out on his forehead and wanted to wipe it away. He was relieved he hadn't given in to the impulse to lie about his name. Somehow, he felt as though this bitch would know.

"Are you wanted by the law?"

That was a painful question, and he swallowed hard. "Not that I know of, ma'am." He tried to grin cheerfully. That wasn't a complete lie, for he didn't believe the burr that clung to his tail for so long could be the law. A lawman would have given up the chase long ago.

"Good," she said crisply. "I do not want the law following you and trespassing on my property. I am the only law here."

Scurlock blinked several times. His earlier estimation of her being tough was too light. He wanted to ask a dozen questions but decided it would be wiser to remain quiet and let her do the talking.

"Perhaps you wouldn't fit the job I have in mind for you." There was a curl to her lip as she went on. "Maybe your principles wouldn't let you take this job."

She was really worked up about something. Scurlock wondered what kind of job she had in mind. He could bet it wouldn't be an ordinary job by the devious way she approached it.

"Never worried much about principles, ma'am," he said easily. "I found out, if I leave them alone, they leave me alone."

He expected his response to bring an acknowledgment of his humor. She ignored his remark completely.

"This job is worth a thousand dollars to me," she said. Those piercing eyes never left Scurlock's face.

Scurlock heard her, but he couldn't believe his ears. His stomach was gone; in its place was one vast hollow. That was a huge sum she offered. For that kind of money, she probably wanted somebody killed. Scurlock didn't flinch at the thought. That part of it didn't bother him, but the aftermath could. He wanted to hear more about this before he accepted. The sum she mentioned pounded in his head. My God! It looked like his luck had finally turned.

"I'd have to know more about the job," he murmured.

Rage washed over her face. This one wasn't used to being crossed in any manner. He spoke up hastily lest she order him out now. "You see, ma'am, I don't want to stir up the law enough to have it coming after me."

That aroused her to an acid mirth, for a faint smile touched her mouth. "There is no law here, except for the law I administer. And I am hiring you. Make up your mind," she said curtly. "Are you interested or not?"

"I'm interested," he said quickly. "I just wanted to learn what you wanted done."

Scurlock suffered her long scrutiny before she spoke. "There is a trespasser on my land," she finally said. "I want that trespasser driven out. Too long I have suffered under this humiliation."

For the first time, Scurlock heard raw passion in her voice. Something personal involved in this, he thought. Caution warned him to proceed slowly. It sounded as though she was up against a force she couldn't handle. Remembering the *vaqueros* he saw riding in here, Scurlock thought that was damned odd. If she couldn't handle this problem with all the help she had, Scurlock couldn't see how a single man could do much about it.

Señora Higuera started to rise. "I see that you are not interested," she said coldly. "Salvio will show you the way out."

"Wait a moment, ma'am," Scurlock protested. "I didn't say that at all. I just wanted a few things cleared up. How many of these trespassers are there?"

The faint, mirthless smile touched her lips again, as she settled back in her chair. "Only two. A woman and her twenty-year-old son." She thought a moment. "They hire an old man to herd the sheep. If they have hired more, I have not heard of it."

Hell, that didn't sound like much of a problem to Scurlock. Why didn't she go ahead and take care of this herself? From what he had seen, she certainly hired enough help.

The Señora's eyes never left Scurlock's face as he pondered. Scurlock couldn't stop the greedy thought from filtering into his mind. Was it possible that she would pay him all at once, even before he did the job? He let the idea slip away. She wouldn't be foolish enough to fall for something like that.

She stirred impatiently, and Scurlock knew the long pause had aroused her anger.

"I was just thinking, señora," he said hastily before she spoke. "Do you have any restrictions on the way I should handle this?"

"Any way you see fit," she said in cold fury. Her eyes looked past him, filled with something only she could see. "Any way you see fit," she repeated. "If they will not be driven out, kill them. Burn their buildings, scatter their sheep." Her voice was becoming shrill and cracked, and both hands were clenched.

My God, Scurlock thought in awe. She really hates this woman, whoever she is. He couldn't help but wonder what the woman had done to Señora Higuera. Somewhere he had read that a woman's hatred was deeper and longer lasting than any man's. From what he had seen and listened to, this woman verified it.

"Yes, or no," she said coldly. "*Dios*, if it takes you this long to make up your mind about a simple decision like this, maybe you are not the man I want."

Scurlock held out a placating hand. "I was just feeling my way, ma'am." He had made up his mind. What she proposed didn't sound so difficult to him. "I need some expense money," he said hesitantly.

"I will give you fifty dollars now. The rest when the job is finished. You will not need more. You can draw on me for necessary supplies."

Scurlock slowly nodded. The amount was far less than he hoped for, but he was better off than when he rode in here a little while ago. "Done," he said. "I'll have to know more about them."

"The woman's name is Marita Higuera." The passion was back in her voice.

She caught the startled flash in Scurlock's eyes and her temper flared. "Do not draw any inferences from the name being the same as mine. The woman is no relation."

Scurlock could not stare her down. She's lying, he thought. It looked as though he had stepped into the middle of a blood feud, and those were the worst kind. He could feel the intensity of her hatred; it literally crackled in the room. He shrugged away the uneasiness his thoughts brought. A man could get hurt stepping into the middle of something like this. Well, it was none of his concern. All he was interested in was getting the money.

"Tell me more about the woman and her son," he said.

Scurlock listened intently while she described them and where they lived. He nodded every now and then. He could see no great obstacles ahead of him.

"This won't be done tomorrow," he warned. "I want to look around a little."

He thought she relaxed for the first time since she began to talk to him. "Take all the time you want." She tried to smile at him, but it was only a baring of her teeth. She wasn't upset; she had something to look forward to.

"I'll need a pair of field glasses," Scurlock said. "And a rifle."

She nodded at each request. "If you think of something else, ask for it." She tapped her teeth with a forefinger as she reflected. "You can sleep in the stables. I see no reason for you to ride all the distance back to town.''

For the first time since he entered this room, Scurlock could grin freely. He rose and started toward the door. A motion of her hand checked him.

''One other thing,'' she said sharply. ''I have three sons. You will meet them later. They are to know nothing of our arrangement.''

Ah, Scurlock thought. So it is a family affair. Her sons are opposed to what she is doing. It surprised him to think that Señora Higuera would bend before anyone. But apparently she feared her sons' shock and anger if they knew. The lying bitch, he thought admiringly. So those same last two names did have some significance.

''Any way you want it, ma'am,'' he said soothingly. After this job was over, he hoped to find another way to keep a hold on her. Damn, he'd be an utter fool to let go of somebody like her. He would have to do some thinking on just how he could do it.

CHAPTER ELEVEN

JONSE LOOKED BACK AT THE burro he led. It plodded along, its head down, its long ears flopping back and forth. But even at that it looked more perky than the horse Jonse rode. Luis was right in saying Ramon was old and tired. Jonse was in no hurry, and he didn't ask Ramon to extend his stride. He intended to return with the burro loaded. When Jonse asked Marita what she needed, she lifted her hands and let them fall helplessly. That said it plainer than anything. She was out of everything. It gave Jonse a free hand to buy whatever he felt was needed.

He shifted in the saddle, needing movement every now and then to ease his stiffness and soreness. But he couldn't complain about his rate of recovery. Each hour, he could swear he was growing stronger. His reflection in the mirror reminded him it was about time he did something about his appearance. A rough-looking character looked back at him. Jonse fingered the beard stubble, scowling at the way he looked. Maybe a beard enhanced some men's appearance; Jonse didn't think it did a thing for him. He turned away from the mirror without shaving, wincing at the thought of the razor pulling against the scabs on his face.

He was content with Ramon's slow pace. Luis had said the town was only five miles away, and even with Ramon's slowness, the town should soon be coming into view. Jonse thought about Marita and Luis as he rode. He wouldn't want to know two finer people. How many people would have put themselves out as they did in saving a stranger's life?

Jonse shook his head as he thought of life's unfairness to some people. All Marita and Luis wanted was to be left alone to make a living. It was the simplest of requests, but Señora Higuera wasn't going to grant them that.

You didn't want any more than that yourself, Jonse thought in a sudden flare of rage. Then that red-headed man came along— He broke off the thought. He had vowed to himself he would not think of that murderer until he was free of his obligation to Marita and Luis. Whether or not he could pick up that trail, he didn't know. He knew only one thing for certain; a man was a fool to look farther ahead than just the day he held in his hands. Maybe it was just as well, Jonse thought soberly. Might scare a man to death, if he could see what was coming at him. He shook his head in restrospection, knowing what he was doing. He was arguing with the way life was, and there was simply no way to win that argument.

"Ramon," he said aloud. "Luis told me to keep my eyes open, or I'd miss the town. We haven't ridden through it yet, have we?"

He smiled at Ramon's soft blubbery snort. Ramon

was trying to tell him that no matter how far away the town was, it was too far. Ramon's tired, old bones had earned all the rest he could get.

Pretty country, Jonse thought absently. Just rolling enough to put an interesting variety in it. Good grazing he thought, noticing the lush vegetation. Support a lot of people, if they could learn to get along together. Jonse's mouth was a straight, pensive line. That probably wouldn't ever happen. Humans had been around for an awful lot of years, and they still clawed and tore at each other.

"We don't learn very much, do we, Ramon? Maybe you animals are a hell of a lot smarter than we are."

Maybe Ramon understood, for that weary snort sounded again.

Jonse had always found it interesting to talk to a horse. Maybe it was because a horse never argued back. "And all those damn-fool humans want is a little peace and ease. They just don't know how to go about getting it." A new fire crept into his voice. "I'll tell you one thing. Marita and Luis are going to get that chance. Nobody's going to bother them."

Jonse grinned as he listened to that snort again.

"There it is, Ramon," he said as the town came into view. "Luis sure was right. If I'd looked away for a few seconds, I'd have miss it."

Counting stores and houses, Jonse would say less than twenty buildings straggled along on each side of the road. A small grouping of humanity in a wilderness, struggling to keep from being swept away into oblivion. If this town had a name, Luis hadn't mentioned it.

They're not having an easy time of it, Jonse thought as he tallied the three stores, and the inevitable cantina. Marita said that Señora Higuera owned the very land these buildings were erected on. From what Jonse could see, the Señora wasn't doing much to make life easier for these people.

He pulled up before the largest of the stores, tied Ramon and the burro, and walked inside. "*Buenos aires*," he greeted the man, dozing in a chair.

The small man's eyes fluttered open, and Jonse caught the startled flash in them. It could be from the alarm of being awakened so abruptly, or the natural wariness the sight of a stranger put into him.

The man bounded to his feet, bobbing his head repeatedly as he rubbed his hands together.

Señor," he apologized. "I did not hear you come in."

Jonse smiled reassuringly at him. "My fault. I just picked the wrong time to come in." That wild animal wariness seemed to be leaving the storekeeper's eyes. Perhaps what he saw in Jonse wasn't enough to build and hold his fright.

"What can I do for you, señor?"

"Just passing through your town and I need a few supplies," Jonse replied. "No better time than now, is there?"

"Never, Señor," the man answered. A gleam filled his eyes.

He's going to rub all the skin off his hands, if he doesn't quit that, Jonse thought. He recognized that gleam. All storekeepers had that shining light at the prospect of business. Jonse would imagine this one didn't too often get a chance to know that eagerness.

"Sí, sí," the man said and swept his hand around the store. "What is in my store is yours. All you have to do is ask."

For a price, Jonse thought sardonically. He would have to be sharp to keep that price fairly reasonable. Very few storekeepers he had known would pass by the opportunity to strip a piece of hide off a stranger. Jonse would have to watch that. He wasn't going to have too large a choice, he thought. Many of the shelves were bare, and others less than half filled. This storekeeper wasn't making his fortune very fast here.

"You got beans and flour?" Jonse asked. "Good," he said to the bobbing head. "Make it a fifty-pound sack of flour and a hundred pounds of beans." He had to keep in mind the burro's and Ramon's carrying capacity.

The storekeeper's eyes opened wide. "Never has Garcia had so much business at one time. Señor, you must be buying for a large family."

"Large enough," Jonse said drily. He wondered if Garcia was the one who had turned Luis down when he tried to buy. If so, Garcia would choke when he learned Jonse was buying for Luis and Marita.

He wandered about the store, picking up several cans as they caught his fancy. Garcia was growing giddy with delight as the order grew on his counter.

Jonse pulled thoughtfully at an earlobe. "Guess that about does it, unless you've got a slab of bacon."

"I have it, I have it," Garcia said in ecstasy. "Is there anything else the Señor desires?"

"I'll need some gunny bags to carry the cans," Jonse said.

"I have them too," Garcia said happily.

Jonse hefted the half-filled bags, estimating their weight. The bags plus the sack of beans should just about load up the burro. Ramon should be able to carry the sack of flour and the slab of bacon.

Garcia whistled as he added up the cost. He beamed as he presented the sum to Jonse, but his eyes were wary. The sum was big enough to bother even him.

Jonse shook his head. "Too bad. I wanted to do business with you. But you're trying to hold me up without a gun." He shrugged. "Oh well, I can buy what I want someplace else in town."

He turned to leave, and Garcia bounded around the counter and seized Jonse's arm. "Señor, if you knew how little I am making. *Dios*, I swear to you I make only a few *centavos*."

Jonse regretfully shook his head. "*Dios* must be frowning at you right now for lying to me."

Garcia paled, then colored. He looked at the figures, then hit himself on the forehead with the heel of his palm. "What a dolt I am. Now I see the mistake I made."

"I thought you would," Jonse said drily. He nodded approval of Garcia's new figure. Garcia had cut a full third off the original price. Jonse might be able to haggle him a little more, but it wouldn't be worth the effort.

Jonse pulled bills and silver out of his pocket to pay for his purchases. Garcia looked at the money in his palm, and his face was radiant.

"I will help you out with this," he said.

"Expected you to," Jonse said and grinned.

Jonse shouldered the sack of beans, balanced it in

place, and winced at the hard thrust of pain the effort cost him. He had a way to go before he was fully back to health. He carried the sack of flour in the other hand. Garcia could manage only one bag of canned goods and the slab of bacon. Jonse would have to return for the second bag.

Garcia chattered away like a parrot until he stepped outside. He looked at Ramon with bulging eyes, and his mouth slowly sagged open.

"I know that horse," he cried. "That is Ramon. He belongs to Luis Higuera."

Jonse chuckled. "I never said he didn't, did I?"

Garcia dropped the bag and bacon to the ground. His face was an angry red. "You have tricked me," he accused Jonse. "You bought all this for that woman and her son."

Jonse's face hardened. "What difference does it make? I paid the price you asked."

Garcia beat his hands together. "But I cannot sell to them. I have promised—" He broke off under Jonse's piercing eyes.

"Because Señora Higuera ordered you not to," Jonse said harshly. "Can you take a breath unless you ask her permission?"

Garcia couldn't meet Jonse's eyes. "I cannot allow this," he protested, his misery evident. "You must take all this back into the store. I will return your money."

Garcia reached for the gunny bag, and Jonse snapped, "You better do some thinking about that. You made a legitimate sale." Those blazing eyes backed up Jonse's words.

"*Dios*," Garcia mourned. "What am I to do?"

"Not much that I can see," Jonse replied. He

placed the sack of beans on the burro's back and tied it firmly. He could balance the two bags of canned goods on either side of the animal.

Garcia's eyes were sick in an ashen face. He followed Jonse back into the store, still seeking words to make this big man change his mind.

"Save your breath," Jonse advised him as he picked up the second bag of canned goods. "See you again, amigo."

"You will not come into my store again," Garcia said shrilly. "I promise you—"

"Horseshit," Jonse said, cutting him short.

He walked outside and finished loading and tying his purchases. He untied Ramon and mounted and grinned at the stricken figure in the doorway. Jonse chuckled as he wondered how Garcia would explain this to Señora Higuera. One thing was certain. He would not make another purchase in Garcia's store. He shrugged the thought away. That was a problem to be faced in the future. This morning's trip had bought more time for Marita and Luis.

CHAPTER TWELVE.

MARITA WAS BIG-EYED AS she watched Jonse and Luis unload the two animals. "Never have I seen so much wealth," she gasped. "You must have bought out Garcia's store."

"I made a dent in it," Jonse said and laughed.

"Garcia didn't know who he was selling to," Luis said, his eyes gleaming with mirth. He stood straighter, and most of the strain was gone from his face. The sight of all these supplies had lifted a tremendous burden from his shoulders.

Jonse helped Luis carry the bags and sacks into the house. He better get out of here as quickly as he could, or he was going to drown in their sea of gratitude.

"Luis, I'd like to go out and look over the place," Jonse said.

He looked back from the doorway. Marita was singing as she put away the supplies. Nothing made a woman feel better than an overabundance of food. Marita was happy. Her singing made Jonse feel good.

This was probably the first time in a long while that Marita had felt like singing.

"Where would you like to go?" Luis asked as he joined Jonse.

"Anywhere you want to take me," Jonse replied.

"I could show you the flock," Luis said hesitantly.

Jonse kept his face straight. A bunch of cattle was called a herd, a number of sheep was a flock. The last thing he wanted to look at was a damned bunch of sheep. He couldn't imagine a more useless waste of time.

"Fine," he said gravely.

"It is not far," Luis said. "Not more than two miles. Hardly worth saddling up for."

Jonse almost snorted in outrage. Walking was unheard of to a cattleman. Hell, he'd walk a half mile to catch up his horse, to ride less than the distance he walked.

Luis watched Jonse anxiously. Jonse could pretend he was still too sore to be walking fool distances like that, but Luis wanted so badly for him to see the sheep.

"Let's go," Jonse said. If a sheepherder could walk that far, a cowman damned well could.

Streak heard them and limped out of the shed. He tried to pick up speed at the sight of Jonse, but the old step simply wasn't there. Jonse wished he could say Streak was better, but he couldn't.

Streak tried to leap on him, and Jonse fended him off. "Down, boy. For a while, you're going to take it easy." Streak had a long way to go before he was fully recovered.

"Can he make it?" Jonse asked Luis.

Luis considered that. "He'd insist upon going

anyway, wouldn't he? We will take it easy. Maybe it will do him more good than harm."

Jonse hoped Luis was right. He glanced sharply at Luis and could read nothing in that face. Maybe Luis's consideration was for Jonse and not the dog. It wasn't necessary, Jonse thought a little stiffly.

Streak didn't want to range out ahead of Jonse, racing back every now and then to announce he had found something interesting. Instead, he stayed close to Jonse's side, seemingly satisfied to move slowly.

Jonse thought of the sheep and asked, "Will he scare the sheep?" Jonse didn't know how Streak would react around sheep. He had never been around the bleating creatures before. But Streak should be easy to whistle down, if he got it into his head to chase the sheep.

"They are used to dogs," Luis answered. He was silent for a dozen strides.

Jonse thought, He has something to say, but he is having trouble finding the words. He didn't prod Luis. If it was important enough, Luis would find the words.

"It has been a long time since I have seen Marita so happy," Luis finally said. "I cannot remember when I last heard her sing. For the first time in a long while, she feels secure. I cannot tell you how much I appreciate what you have done for us."

"Then don't try," Jonse said bluntly. "If I remember right, you and Marita cut me off pretty short when I tried to say some thanks."

Luis's eyes flashed, and for a moment, Jonse thought he was offended. He relaxed when he saw the corners of Luis's mouth twitching.

Luis could no longer control his mirth. It broke out into full laughter. "In many ways, you remind me of Bernal. He always advised me that when one has something to say, he should say it without beating around the bush. It clears the air so much faster. It is so. The air is cleared between us. We agree to say nothing more about our mutual debts. But I will not forget."

"That makes a pair of us," Jonse returned. Bernal must have been a wise man in many ways. The only trouble was that Bernal couldn't apply that wisdom to his personal affairs.

They walked through luxuriant grass, and Jonse reached down and plucked a handful of it. "Grama, isn't it? We've got it in Texas, but I've never seen a better stand. Stock should do well on it."

"They do," Luis replied. The tightness was returning to his face. "I would ask nothing more, if we could only be left alone. We could handle the predators and the weather. We know how to combat the sickness in the animals. We could prosper, if only—" He sighed and didn't finish.

Jonse nodded. Luis was talking about people's interference, the toughest to stop or turn aside. "Maybe that can be stopped too, Luis," he said softly.

"*Dios*, I hope so," Luis muttered.

Jonse tossed his handful of grass into the air. Grama cured well on the ground, making an excellent hay. He wished his own small ranch was covered with this grass. Soon, Jonse would have to talk to Señora Higuera and point out some facts that it was best to live and let live. It all depended upon how far the Señora was prepared to go and how much force she intended to use.

"Bernal taught me many things," Luis went on. "He was positive that it would be easier for a few people to make a living with sheep than cattle."

Jonse nodded his agreement. That explained why Bernal who had been a cattleman had stocked this place with sheep. Cattle took far more help to run than a boy and a woman could supply.

"Bernal used this place as an experimental range," Luis went on. "He stocked it with two hundred Merinos brought from Vermont. Those are sheep originally brought from France. They are noted for their long, curly wool. But Bernal wasn't satisfied with that. He crossed those Merinos with the light shearing Mexican breeds. The effect was magical. Instead of two pounds of fleece, six to eight pounds of wool were shorn. In place of lambs producing eight-pound carcasses and wethers twenty-five to thirty, fat sheep yielded thirty-five to forty pounds dressed. *Dios*, how the news of the sheep we were raising spread. Stockmen from all over New Mexico came to purchase breeding stock from us."

Luis face was more animated than Jones had ever seen it.

"Our ewes were bringing five to ten dollars apiece. An excellent ram brought almost any price we cared to ask for it. Then all that trade dried up after Bernal died." Luis's face darkened. "I am sure people were warned to no longer trade with us."

"Probably," Jonse grunted. From the little he had heard of Señora Higuera, she was a vindictive woman. "You still have the good breeding stock, haven't you? That trade will come back." Jonse didn't know how that trade could be brought back, but a lot of things were going to change, if he had anything to say about it.

"How many head do you have now, Luis?"

"Almost five hundred," Luis responded.

The figure surprised Jonse. This grass was good. Three thousand acres would support a far greater number than Luis mentioned.

Luis guessed at Jonse's thoughts, for he said, "Our numbers should be larger. But in the past few months we have lost too many head. Not to disease or natural predators. We have lost them to human wolves. I have found where horsemen have driven small bands of our sheep over a ravine. Other small bands have been slaughtered with guns and knives." He tried to smile, and it was a painful effort. "It is hard to build up your numbers when such a force is against you."

Jonse could understand Luis's despondency. It was tough enough to fight against the attrition caused by weather and predators without the cunning viciousness of man against you. Jonse would have thought Señora Higuera was a more clever woman than this. Destroying Marita's and Luis's markets was a certain way to drive them to ruin, even though a little slow. But evidently, Eulalia Higuera's impatience was driving her to use more drastic methods. She had tremendous influence in this part of the country; Jonse had seen evidence of that in Garcia's store this morning. His eyes darkened as he thought he had a lot of convincing to do to make Señora Higuera see the error of her ways.

Luis's despondency deepened. "While Bernal was alive, he saw that nothing of this kind ever happened to us. But now—" He spread his hands in that familiar gesture of defeat. "The Señora is a powerful woman. She breaks anybody who crosses her like that." Luis made the motion of breaking a stick.

"Get that hopelessness off your face, Luis," Jonse ordered. "Maybe this time, she's found a stick too tough to break."

"I hope so," Luis said fervently, but his face didn't brighten to any appreciable degree.

Jonse had been watching that odd-looking construction ahead of them for the last few minutes. At first, he thought it was some kind of a holding corral, but if so, this was the funniest-looking one he had ever seen. He didn't ask any questions until he reached it. He should have enough brains to figure this out for himself.

He looked at a long, narrow chute, widening out into a circular space, all of it fenced. A small pond of oily liquid filled the circular space. Beyond the pond was a small platform, tilted back toward the pond. Some kind of a dipping vat, Jonse decided. That certainly wasn't just water in the pond.

Luis confirmed Jonse's guess. "Yes, a dipping vat. Bernal had it built when I was not much higher than this." He held his hand waist-high. "He had stonemasons quarry rock and build it. The solution is all ready when we find evidence of scab in the sheep."

"You do not know what scab is?" Luis asked, seeing no enlightenment on Jonse's face. "It is one of the curses of a sheepman's life, until a way was found to control it. Scab is caused by a tiny mite. It takes a very keen eye to see them. The mite irritates the sheep's skin, and he rubs himself raw to ease the itching. Then a scab forms over the raw places. Bernal told me he had seen some sheep an entire mass of scab. It is also highly infectious."

Jonse was interested in anything that fought animal disease. "Does it kill the sheep?"

"I have not seen many of them actually die," Luis answered. "But in extreme cases, I have no doubt they could. A sheep is a stubborn creature. It can lie down and die for no apparent reason. Scab makes the animal listless. It will not eat, and it loses weight rapidly. The wool is affected, and is almost worthless."

"What's the cure?" Jonse asked.

"Usually sulphur and lime. Sometimes tobacco is used, but it has been difficult to get tobacco in the quantities we need. Lately, I have not been able to buy sulphur, and no wagon will haul it for me, if I can find it. There are rocks on Señora Higuera's property that can be burned to get lime and lye. I do not dare go onto her land after them." He looked broodingly at the dipping vat. "This is all the solution I have on hand. So far, I have the scab under control. But if it breaks out anew, I do not know what I will do."

Jonse didn't let pity show on his face, but he felt it. Poor Luis was hemmed in from all sides.

"The sheep are driven through the chute," Jonse asked, "and pushed into the solution? How deep is it?"

"Considerably deeper than an animal is tall. He goes completely under and has to swim to the platform, where the excess solution drips back into the pool. Believe me, every drop is precious from now on."

Jonse could imagine that without being told.

Luis's face cleared. "Ah, I hear the sheep. They are just ahead."

Streak moved closer to Jonse and nuzzled his hand.

"You see that vat, Streak?" Jonse asked. "The next time you get to itching, I'll put you through there."

Streak whined as though he understood the threat.

The sheep were grazing in a little bowl. In places the grass was tall enough to almost cover the lambs' heads. Jonse saw dozens of them, some of them bounding and racing about in play, others sedately trailing after their mothers.

"Must have been a good lamb crop," he commented.

"Excellent," Luis said. "We do not dare go much beyond this point. From sad experience, I know what will happen to my sheep if they are found on Señora Higuera's property."

The sheep must have known that Jonse was a stranger, for as he and Luis continued toward them, excited bleating broke out all over. But instead of scattering, they raced to bunch together, crowding tightly.

"Do they always bunch up like that when they're startled?" Jonse asked.

"Always," Luis replied. "You are thinking of the way cattle scatter under like circumstances. No, sheep are much easier to handle. One herder and a dog can handle two thousand head with no difficulty."

"Well, I've learned one good thing about the critters," Jonse said. "I'll bet you have to move them constantly to keep them from ruining the grass."

"An old cattleman's belief," Luis said and smiled. "Perhaps in dry, light, thin soil sheep may destroy the sod with their sharp hoofs. Close feeding may harm the grass in poor soil, but it is not so where the earth is strong and deep. There, sheep do not pull grass out by the roots, and their small hoofs harrow in the seed, planting it deeper. They manure the soil, improving it for both grazing and farming." He smiled at the skepticism on Jonse's face. "Look at this grass. Do you see where it is going thin?"

Jonse had to admit he couldn't see any weak spots.

"The sheep are penned up at night for protection against the wild animals. They are turned out at daylight, and the herder keeps in front of the flock, instead of behind them. That way, he keeps the fast sheep back and enables poor or weak ones to keep up. As the sheep approached him the herder gradually falls back to slow their movements. By noon, he has reached the water hole where he allows the sheep to water. Then he lets them shade up under trees from one to three hours, after which he takes them back to camp by a different route from the one traveled in the morning. He covers a total of about six miles, not penning up the sheep again until the sun sets."

Jonse grunted. This was interesting, but Luis was not speaking of the pressure on the grass. From the looks of the grass, Jonse would say the sheep had been grazing only a few days.

"For a month, they have been traveling the same six miles," Luis said quietly. "Soon the herder will move the flock to another route to let this grass recover."

Jonse whistled softly. Luis wasn't exaggerating.

Jonse couldn't find any fault with the sheep on this grass.

They had been walking as they talked, and Jonse was quite close before he spotted a motionless figure, standing in the shade of a tree. That must be the herder, for he grinned at Jonse's startled expression and lifted his hand in greeting.

Luis introduced them. "Jonse, this is Pancho. He already knows you, though he has never spoken to you. I told you he helped me when you were hurt."

Pancho extended a horny hand. "*Dios*," he said softly. "He is even bigger than I remember. My pleasure, señor," he said as he clasped Jonse's hand. "You look as though you have fully recovered." He shook his head at a memory. "I would not have bet on you when I first saw you."

Jonse chuckled. "I wouldn't have bet on me either when I first saw my reflection in a mirror. Señor, my deepest appreciation—"

Pancho cut him short with a wave of his hand. "*Por nada*," he said, wiping out all necessity for more words.

Jonse judged Pancho to be in his seventies. Pancho's face was lined and seamed, and his shoulders were bowed under his years. But his eyes were still clear and aware of what went on about him.

A furious barking turned Jones's head. A dog was racing toward them, barking its displeasure at the intrusion of two strangers, Jonse and Streak. Part collie, Jonse thought, as he reached down and secured his hold on the nape of Streak's neck.

"I don't want Streak tangling with your dog," he said. "Not in the shape he is in." Ordinarily, Jonse would have no doubt about Streak's ability to take care of himself, but right now, he was in a poor position to defend himself.

"They will not fight," Pancho said calmly. "Lupe is a female."

Jonse let go of Streak. Streak knew this was a female long before Jonse did. The growling had changed to an eager whining. "You behave yourself," he admonished Streak.

Lupe and Streak touched noses, then Lupe raced about him, barking her approval. Every now and then, she darted in to touch noses again, then raced out of Streak's reach. Jonse ached for Streak as the dog tried to respond to the open invitation, but he moved stiffly, and he could not begin to catch up with Lupe.

Jonse watched Streak's endeavors to catch the female. Maybe this would do Streak good and help him to loosen up his stiffened muscles.

"Two different breeds," he commented. "And already friends. It's too bad that humans can't learn from animals."

Pancho bobbed his head. "It is *verdad*, amigo. But of course her being a female and him a male helps," he added drily.

Jonse laughed until tears came into his eyes. This was a wise old man. In just his short acquaintance, he liked the old herder.

"No trouble, Pancho?" Luis asked.

"No trouble, Luis," Pancho shrugged. "None since last week when I found a dozen head shot." A barely perceptible shiver ran through him. "But a bad feeling is in the air."

Luis nodded gravely. He knew what Pancho meant. "You have seen none of them?"

"If I never see a Higuera again, it will suit me fine," Pancho growled. "Would you like to see the sheep?"

"At Luis's nod, Pancho picked up a long stick leaning against a tree, and moved out ahead of him. For his age, he had a surprisingly fluid motion in his gait.

"The best herder we ever had," Luis said in a low voice to Jonse before they followed Pancho. "He used to work for the Higueras. Señora Higuera had him flogged for something that offended her."

"The more I hear about her, the more I find out what a lovable woman she is," Jonse said. "You're lucky to have Pancho, Luis."

"How well I know it," Luis replied.

They followed and caught up with Pancho. The sheep were over their initial fright at the appearance of a stranger, or it could be that Pancho's presence told the sheep that nothing could be wrong, for they had gone back to their grazing.

Pancho's face was alive with enthusiasm as he pointed out the finger points of an individual animal. His love for his charges was apparent.

Jonse couldn't share Pancho's enthusiasm. He couldn't see a damned bit of difference in any of them. To him, sheep were just stupid, noisy animals. But he had to admit the lambs had an appeal of their own. One of them, showing not the slighest fear, came closer and closer to Jonse. Jonse leaned over, extending his fingers. The lamb touched them with his nose, then bounded back. He cocked his head from one side to the other, then decided there was no harm for him. He came back, and in the next instant, the lamb was sucking Jonse's fingers.

"Look at the little devil," Jonse said, turning his head toward Luis. "He's not in the least scared of me."

Jonse heard the savage rush of small hoofs, he was positive that was alarm on Luis's face.

"Look out," Luis yelled.

Jonse barely had time to straighten when a tremendous force smashed into his butt, sending him sprawling. His face plowed through the grass. He rolled over, raised his head, and spit out shreds of grass.

A ram stood not ten feet from Jonse, its head down, its forehoofs slashing the grass in rage. Jonse could swear the damned thing's eyes were red, and it was getting ready to charge again.

Pancho moved with surprising quickness. He leaped toward the ram and brought his stick down smartly across its neck. "*Vamos*," he yelled. He was as angry as the ram. "Is this the way you treat our amigo?"

Another whack made up the ram's mind, and it whirled and trotted off, shaking its head in unspent anger.

Luis rushed to Jonse and helped him to his feet. "Are you hurt?" he asked anxiously.

Pancho was just as anxious. "It is all my fault, amigo. I should have cut out old Rufino a week ago and put him with the other rams." He shook his head mournfully. "But I put it off. Do not blame him too harshly. He was afraid you meant harm to one of his little ones."

"Are you sure you are all right?" Luis asked again.

Jonse took a tentative step, and his legs worked all

right, but he felt bruised all over. That damned ram had an awful lot of power. He took another step, grunting as he did so. "Rufino, huh? You named him well. He's rough all right."

The anxiety remained in Luis's face, and Jonse managed a wry grin. "Nothing broken, except my dignity." He glared at Luis and Pancho. If he wasn't mistaken, their lips were beginning to twitch. "By God," he said wrathfully. "I'd like to butcher him and have him served for supper tonight. I don't like mutton, but I'd enjoy eating him."

Pancho and Luis could no longer contain their mirth. They wrapped their arms around each other and howled with laughter.

"Funny, is it?" Jonse said furiously. "I wish you two had your asses busted by him."

"It has happened to us several times," Luis managed to gasp out between peals of laughter. "Amigo, we do not want to laugh at you. But you looked so funny sailing through the air. And the way your face looked when you spit out the grass." Laughter overcame him again, and he could no longer talk.

Jonse had to grin. "I guess it was funny," he conceded. "But I wish you two had gotten busted instead of me. Just when I was ready to think of damned sheep more kindly," he finished plaintively.

That brought on new howls of laughter, and Jonse waited for it to die down. "I never knew sheep could be so dangerous," he said ruefully. "I know better now."

Pancho wiped the tears from his eyes. "Amigo, you will do. I have learned to trust a man who can laugh at himself. You will come again?" he asked.

"Only after I check to see that Rufino isn't

around," Jonse replied. "Sure, I'll be back."

"Are you sure you can make it?" Luis asked. "I could go and bring back Ramon, or the wagon."

Jonse's vulgar expletive erased all of Luis's doubts about his being able to make the walk.

Pancho stopped Luis before he and Jonse started away. "We are running short on salt, Luis," he said gravely.

Luis sighed. "I know it, Pancho. I'll try to do something about it."

Pancho's face showed how much he hated to heap more trouble on Luis's head. "This morning I found several grubs in the sheep's head. It must be taken care of immediately."

"That can be handled easily enough," Luis said wearily.

Luis walked away with Jonse, glancing covertly at him every now and then.

"Forget it," Jonse said brusquely. "I'm not hurting." He stopped and whistled for Streak. He had to repeat the whistle several times before Streak reluctantly broke away from Lupe.

"Streak will be back again," Jonse said as he waited for the dog to join him. He will be back again, if I let him." He reached down and patted Streak's head. "Did you make an impression on her, you old devil?"

Streak's tongue lolled out, and he waggled his tail.

"You know I think this has done him a lot of good," Jonse remarked.

Luis's face didn't lighten. "It did not do me any good," he said heavily. "You heard what Pancho said about the salt?"

"Salt that much of a problem?" Jonse asked.

Luis made a disparaging motion with his hand. "Ordinarily, no. It takes about three gallons of salt mixed with a few pounds of ashes and sulphur. The sheep are salted once a week. If salt was available, I would not give it another thought. But I cannot buy it in town. The next source is some fifty miles. I cannot think of leaving Marita while I drive that far."

No wonder Luis looked so depressed. "Those grubs Pancho spoke about. Is that as big a problem?"

Luis shook his head. "No. A few pints of soot, taken from the stove or chimney will take care of that."

Jonse was afraid Luis and Marita were running a ragtag operation. He suspected that money was short. Inability to get supplies only complicated the problem.

He cleared his throat, hesitating to ask such a personal question. "Luis, is this a profitable operation?"

Luis looked momentarily surprised, then he said proudly, "We netted over two thousand dollars last year."

Jonse whistled. That was a neat profit, an amount that several ranches he knew of couldn't match.

"Life would be good," Luis said and sighed. "If only—" He stared off into space and didn't finish.

Jonse didn't know what he could do about that "if" at the moment, but he knew he was going to do something.

CHAPTER THIRTEEN

SCURLOCK LOWERED THE GLASSES and rubbed his eyes. He had been watching the house for quite a while. Twice, he had seen the woman come out on some errand, then go back in. He was convinced she was alone. It should be no great problem to drive these people off this land the Señora wanted.

He levered a shell into the rifle and patiently waited. Sooner or later, the woman would appear again. A good scare might frighten her into leaving. If a more drastic lesson was needed, Scurlock was ready to deliver that, too.

He lay on a small hill, some two hundred yards from the small house, basking in the weak fall sun. The little house he had been watching certainly didn't compare with the one Señora Higuera ran. Scurlock had been all over the land Señora Higuera described as belonging to that woman. He grinned wolfishly. This Marita woman was a damned fool to try and buck the Señora.

Scurlock had infinite patience, but he was beginning to shift uncomfortably as time dragged by. Wasn't that fool woman ever coming out again?

Scurlock intended giving her just a warning, a convincing suggestion that she would be smart to abandon this place as fast as she could. If the first warning wasn't enough, then there was that flock of sheep and the lone sheepherder he had seen earlier this morning. Maybe that sheepherder was Marita's son. Or it could have been the sheepherder the Señora mentioned. At the moment, it didn't make any difference.

Scurlock's eyes gleamed as the woman appeared again. She walked to the woodpile, gathered up an armload of sticks and turned back toward the house.

Scurlock snugged the rifle butt to his shoulder and waited until the woman was about to step into the house. He squeezed the trigger, aiming for the doorjamb. He didn't need the glasses to see if he had hit his target. He knew what kind of marksman he was.

The report of the rifle was sharp and distinct, its echoes rolling across the quiet land. The woman flung up her arms, throwing sticks in all directions, then ducked hastily into the shelter of the house.

The wolfish grin returned to Scurlock's face. That should scare the hell out of her. He moved the rifle sights and deliberately shot out a window. From this distance, he couldn't hear the shattering of the glass, but it would be frighteningly loud to anybody inside the house. Scurlock could imagine the woman cowering inside, and the thought delighted him.

He slithered off the hilltop and made his way to his horse, tethered a good mile away. This was the kind of job he liked, requiring only a minimum of effort. It was too bad that jobs like this one happened so damned rarely.

Jonse and Luis were talking sheep as they approached the house. Jonse would never have believe he could become so interested in the subject. Luis could talk learnedly about the animals. Bernal had taught him well.

"Go to the shed, Streak," Jonse ordered the dog. He didn't know how Marita felt about dogs, but Marcia never wanted Streak in the house, no matter how much she loved him. Jonse could agree with her. A man made enough work for a woman without adding a dog.

He turned his head to grin at Luis, and Luis was staring frozenly at the front of the house. For a moment, Jonse didn't see what caught Luis's attention, but there was no mistaking the strain in his expression. "What is it, Luis?"

"*Dios*," Luis burst out. "The window is broken."

Jonse saw it then. Most of the pane had shattered, leaving a large shard hanging from an upper corner. He swore softly at his blindness. He was sure the window was intact when he left the house earlier. "Now how in the hell did that happen?"

If Luis heard him, he didn't answer. He raced for the house, calling, "Madre," at the top of his lungs.

Jonse shook his head and followed him. Luis was drawing a grimmer conclusion from the broken window than Jonse felt. Any one of a dozen mishaps could account for the shattered glass.

Marita came out of the doorway and ran toward Luis. "If you knew how relieved I am to see you." She threw her arms about Luis.

Jonse hurried toward them. "What's this all about?" he demanded.

Marita was distraught, though she hadn't panicked. But something unusual had happened. It was written in the thinness of Marita's lips, in the paleness of her face.

Luis was more upset than his mother, and she tried to comfort him. "It is all right, Luis. Nothing further happened, though I was frightened. Somebody shot the window out."

Jonse's eyes sharpened. He wasn't discounting what Marita said, yet he couldn't help being dubious. A bullet usually went through glass, leaving a clean hole without shattering it. But he wasn't enough of an authority to say that was always an absolute result. Maybe it depended upon the angle of the bullet.

"You're sure, Marita?" He hadn't intended that skepticism to be so pronounced in his voice.

Marita bridled at his tone. "You do not believe me," she challenged. "Whoever it was also shot at me just as I was entering the house. Come, I will show you."

Luis glared at Jonse for arguing with Marita, and Jonse shook his head at him. He didn't want wrought-up nerves making either of them reach a hasty decision. Luis's face didn't change. Without further investigation, he believed what Marita said.

Marita led Jonse to the doorway and pointed out the splintered, gouged-out hole in the doorjamb. "Now you can tell me that a squirrel made that hole."

"Sorry, Marita," Jonse said quietly. He pulled a knife from his pocket, opened the big blade, and dug about in the hole. The knife point grated on something metallic, a few inches into the jamb.

It took Jonse several minutes to dig out the slug. He bounced it in his hand. The lead slug was misshapen by the impact against the wood, but not enough to mistake it for anything else but a bullet. ''A rifle bullet,'' Jonse said tersely. ''The bullet that shattered the window should be somewhere in the room.''

It took several moments for Jonse to locate another hole head-high in the plastered wall. He eyed the second hole thoughtfully. ''Did you see who it was?''

Luis's face was a pasty gray. ''He tried to kill you,'' he gasped.

Jonse glanced sharply at Luis. Luis wouldn't be of much help at the moment.

Marita helplessly shook her head. ''I did not see him. I was too frightened to spend time looking around. I only wanted to get inside the house.''

''Sure,'' Jonse said gently. His hand rested on her shoulder. She was made of tough stuff. Jonse had known other women who would have become hysterical in situations like this.

''I don't think he was trying to hit you, Marita. Somebody just wanted to give you a warning. Do I dare name the one I'm thinking of?''

''I can think of no other,'' Marita whispered.

Jonse nodded. ''Señora Higuera. She probably sent one of her sons to give you the warning. I think I better go over and have a talk with them.'' He turned to leave the room, and Marita clutched his arm.

''You cannot involve yourself in this,'' she cried. ''That would only turn her anger on you.

Jonse grinned at her. ''I've had others mad at me before. Luis, can I use Ramon again?''

Luis was slowly regaining his normal color. ''I go with you,'' he said, his eyes flashing.

An exploding temper was the last thing Jonse needed now. He wanted to take a cautious step at a time until he was on more solid ground.

"No," he said. At the fierce disappointment molding Luis's face he said, "You would leave Marita at a time like this?"

The reproof took all the blaze out of Luis's eyes. "I am so mad and scared I cannot think. You are right." He walked to the door with Jonse, turned his head toward Marita, and said, "I will be right back."

Worry made Marita look years older. "Jonse," she begged. "Please be careful."

"I will," Jonse said softly. Her worry was all for him. It made him feel warm all over.

Luis gave Jonse directions to the Higuera hacienda, as Jonse saddled Ramon. Cribber nickered a protest at his inactivity, and Jonse took time to soothe him. "Soon, boy," he promised.

Jonse led Ramon out of the shed, and Luis looked up at him after he mounted. "I can only repeat what Marita said. "Be careful."

Jonse grinned lazily at Luis. "I'm not going over there to stir up trouble. I'm only trying to calm it down."

Luis's expression didn't change. Jonse wasn't fooling him. "Yes," he said heavily. "And our debt grows larger."

"Don't fret about it," Jonse said.

He looked back after he rode fifty yards. Luis hadn't moved, and Marita stood in the doorway. Their worry about him was almost a tangible thing. Good people, he thought. They would not relax until he returned.

Jonse found the lane leading to the Higuera house with no difficulty. Luis had said it would be nearly five miles to the hacienda. From here, Jonse couldn't afford to relax a moment. He could run into violent opposition at any step.

He hadn't ridden a mile when he saw a rider approaching him. Ah, he thought, and sighed. He had been spotted. Did this rider come to stop him from going farther? Any way he wants it, Jonse thought as he pulled up and waited for the rider to reach him.

He's had everything his way, Jonse thought, as the rider pulled up before him. That cold face was chiseled in patrican lines, and there wasn't the slightest welcome in the eyes or mouth. This man was used to the best; it showed in his clothing and in the silver-mounted trappings of his horse. But Jonse thought there was a weakness beneath that haughty surface. The chin was too weak, and the mouth wasn't quite steady. The weakness was almost an aroma Jonse could smell. Was this man capable of shooting near a defenseless woman in an effort to frighten her? Jonse meant to find out.

He made no effort to greet the rider, staring at him with equally cold eyes. Was that apprehension behind that barely perceptible trembling in the lips? It was possible. If so, a guilty feeling could nurture that apprehension.

"Señor, you are on private property," the man said. His voice was too high-pitched, and Jonse thought. He's scared of something.

"Who says so?" Jonse drawled. He sat in the saddle, looking indolent, but his hand was near his holstered gun. He wasn't surprised at the wash of color across the man's face. It told Jonse that temper was very close to the surface. This one wasn't used to being crossed in any way.

"I, Andras Higuera, say so," Higuera said passionately. "My madre owns this land you are now on. She does not allow strangers on it."

Jonse's indolent posture changed. "Then you'll do," he snapped. "I am a friend of Marita and Luis Higuera." That brought a different reaction than Jonse expected. If anything, Andras Higuera showed relief.

"You are not the American law?" That could be a small quaver in Higuera's voice.

This is interesting, Jonse thought. Why is he so fearful of the American law?

"I am not." Jonse's tone was as crisp as the popping of a whip. "But that doesn't mean I can't protect Marita and Luis. This morning somebody fired too close to Marita, then shot out one of her windows."

An angry flush mottled Higuera's place. "You are accusing me of this?" he shouted.

"Not yet," Jonse said drily. "I'm just warning you not to try something like that again. I know what your mother thinks of Marita. She paid an unfriendly call on her the other morning."

Higuera looked as though he were choking. His mouth worked, but for a moment, he could make no sound. "You insult my dignity," he finally managed to say. He worked himself up into a high rage. "Why do you think we should have any interest in two ragpickers?"

"Ah, stop it," Jonse said wearily. "You're not fooling yourself, let alone me. I'm just telling you, if you're smart, you'll leave Marita and Luis alone."

He stabbed a finger at Higuera's face. "If you don't believe I mean what I'm saying, all you have to do is test me."

Jonse watched curiously as the thin veneer stripped away from Higuera's temper. Temper was a volatile thing, it could flare up into uncontrollable passion, or it could simmer for a long time before it finally became uncontrollable. This could be the moment. Higuera was armed. He could have this any way he wanted.

"You cannot talk to me like this," Higuera screamed.

Jonse locked eyes with him. "I just did," he said acidly. "If you people are smart, you'll let them alone."

For a long moment, Jonse watched Higuera's struggle for control. His eyes never left Higuera's hand, but Higuera made no move toward his gun.

"Get off our land," Higuera said. His harsh breathing made his voice jerky.

"You can order me off," Jonse agreed. "But don't forget what I said." He started to add something more, then held his words. He had already made his point. There was no advantage in belaboring the point further.

Jonse slowly turned Ramon, his back tensing. He dared not show a lack of confidence in himself.

Jonse never looked back as he rode away, but he didn't draw a free breath until he was better than a hundred yards away. He wasn't surprised to find moisture on his forehead. But he could believe Higuera would remember what he said to him. He would have to wait and see if events proved him right or wrong.

Andras Higuera watched until the horseman was out of sight. His breathing was under control, though he still felt shaky inside. *Dios*, he had looked into those blazing eyes, and they had looked like the pits of hell. He didn't know what connection this stranger had with Marita and Luis, but he must be very close to them.

Andras suddenly slammed his fist against the horn. He promised himself that this one would never talk to him again in such a vein. Andras did not doubt that the shooting had taken place. But who had done it? Surely, neither of his brothers. He sucked in a hard breath. The new man his mother had hired; that had to be the logical answer. He had tried to argue against his mother when he first heard she hired a new hand, but she shouted him down, saying furiously that she knew what she was doing.

Andras groaned at the thought of facing his mother's anger again. But he must. She had to be made to see the danger of what she was doing. This one he had just confronted wasn't the American law, but if there were additional violence, the next new arrival could readily be the law. She must be made to see that. Andras hit the horn again, but he couldn't arouse the anger he wanted to back him up.

"*Dios*," he groaned. "Why must it be so?" He could find no answer to that. But life could be so pleasant, if only his mother was content to let things be. Yes, he must try to talk to her again, but the sinking hollow in his stomach told him how futile it would be.

CHAPTER FOURTEEN

SCURLOCK LEANED AGAINST a wall just beside the
closed door. He was on his second cigarette, and this
one was getting short. The Señora and her oldest son
were having one hell of a fight. As hard as Scurlock
tried, he couldn't make out enough of the words to
tell what the argument was about. He was afraid it
could be about him. Andras didn't like Scurlock, and
that dislike was poorly disguised every time he
looked Scurlock's way. At first, Andras's dislike
amused Scurlock. Andras didn't want his mother's
judgment being influenced by a stranger. But the
length of this meeting tonight worried Scurlock.
Señora Higuera had sent word to Scurlock that she
wanted to see him, but the long wait disturbed him. If
the argument was over him, it could mean that Andras was winning.

Scurlock threw down the cigarette butt and
crushed it under his boot as he heard footsteps approaching the door. That sounded as though the argument were over.

The door opened, and Andras made a last, desperate plea. "Madre, listen."

"I will listen no more, Señora Higuera said coldly. "I know what I am doing. You will say no more about it. understand?"

Andras turned the other way as he came out of the room and didn't see Scurlock. Scurlock caught just a glimpse of Andras's profile. From what he saw, Andras wasn't happy at all.

Scurlock grinned crookedly as he listened to the hard pound of Andras's boot heels against the polished floor, indicating how angry Andras was. It was apparent that Andras had lost.

Scurlock tapped discreetly on the door after Andras was out of sight.

"Yes?"

Scurlock winced at the familiar bite in that voice. The Señora was furious, and Scurlock felt as though he walked on the brink of a precipice.

"Scurlock, ma'am," he said apologetically. "You wanted to see me?"

"Come in," the voice said.

Scurlock grimaced as he opened the door and stepped inside. He had the strong feeling he was involved in the argument that had taken place, and he didn't know what he faced when he stepped into the room. The last time he was here, he had sat down without being invited. But now there was a subtle change, and he felt it. He stood before Señora Higuera, trying to keep the worry from showing on his face.

She had the eyes of a hunting cat. Scurlock had noticed the mercilessness in them before. He wished he could read the thoughts behind those eyes.

"So you were outside the door when Andras left," she said flatly.

Scurlock could deny that, but he decided the best thing for him to tell the truth. "Yes, ma'am." He dared to venture an opinion. "He looked like he was plumb upset."

Her face twisted, and Scurlock thought he had gone too far. "I didn't hear what the argument was about," Scurlock said hastily.

Now he was certain he'd gone too far, and he wished he'd kept his mouth shut. He had never seen such malevolence in a woman's eyes, and he thought she was going to scream at him, for her mouth opened.

It looked as though she changed what she intended saying, for she said impatiently, "What we argued about does not matter. Andras will not bring it up again. What are you doing to accomplish the job we agreed upon?"

Scurlock looked aggrieved. Damn it, did she expect him to rush in without a preliminary survey? He had already started, hadn't he?

He had to take that weighing look off her face, and he relished telling Señora Higuera about this morning's incident. He chuckled as he described Marita's frightened flight. "Then I shot out her window," he finished triumphantly.

Scurlock expected praise, and he was startled by her words.

"I know all about that," she said furiously.

How in the hell could she? Scurlock wondered. He could swear that no one had seen him anyplace around Marita's house this morning. He wanted to swear at the logical explanation. Andras had seen him and rushed to Señora Higuera to tell her. But he could take encouragement in thinking that had been the basis of the argument between the Señora and her son. Hadn't she shut up Andras? If Scurlock's surmise was right, it meant that Señora Higuera was still behind him.

Eulalia stared at him. She debated briefly about telling him that Andras said Marita had hired a new man, an American, then decided against it. She did not know how Scurlock would react. The news could scare him off finishing the job, thinking the odds were now too great. He could withdraw, and she could not risk that. No, she wanted Scurlock to go ahead and finish his work.

"You shot out a window and frightened a woman," she said contemptuously. "Does it change anything? She is still there."

Her tone stung Scurlock, and his face stiffened. He started to say something in his own defense, but she didn't give him the chance.

"That is not enough," she said angrily. "I did not expect it to take forever. I want this done now."

Scurlock stared at the floor to keep Eulalia from seeing the rage in his eyes. "That was only my opening move," he said sullenly. "Tonight, I'll—"

Again, she stopped him. "I do not want to hear about it. The only thing I want to hear is that it is done."

"You will," Scurlock said savagely. He wished he could fling this job in her face, but the thought of the money he could collect was too much for him. This woman had had things her way for far too long. She had complete dominion over her sons, and she expected to hold the same control over him. Oh God, if he could only think of something that would cut her down to size. But that was a luxury he couldn't afford to think about now.

"You'll hear," he snapped and spun on his heel. He did not look back as he walked to the door, but he knew the Señora's eyes never left him. He could feel them boring into his back.

Scurlock swung down and walked to the small hut. He had spotted the shepherd's living quarters earlier. A light was on in the window. The shepherd hadn't yet gone to bed.

Scurlock moved toward the hut on noiseless feet, but even as careful as he was, it did not prevent the dog from hearing him. The animal stood at the doorway, barking its fool head off.

Scurlock wished he dared shoot the damned dog to shut up its barking, but a shot wasn't the wisest thing.

"Lupe," a man's voice called. "What is it?"

Scurlock shook his head. There was no longer any chance of reaching the hut undetected. "Ho, there," he called. "Anybody home?"

A figure appeared beside the barking dog. "Quiet, Lupe," he shouted. "Si, señor. I am here."

Scurlock openly approached the hut. He had seen that damned dog earlier, but he hadn't made any plans to dispose of it. That was going to have to be taken care of.

The dog kept barking despite its owner's rebuke. The sound was like a piece of broken glass scraping over Scurlock's skin. Did a dog have an instinct for menace? It could be so, Scurlock thought.

Scurlock was close enough now to make out the man's figure. The light was behind him, and Scurlock couldn't clearly make out his face, but the slight figure and the bent shoulders told him it was the same one he had observed earlier.

"My horse went lame," Scurlock said. "I had to leave it a piece back. I thought I was lost until I saw your light. Jesus, I could use a cup of coffee."

"I am Pancho," the voice said. "I live here." He cackled in amusement. "It is a good thing you saw my light. It is a long way to another. Come in, come in. The coffee is still warm."

Pancho stepped aside for Scurlock to enter. The dog had never ceased barking. "Lupe, must I beat you?" Pancho shouted at her. "She is suspicious of all strangers," he apologized to Scurlock.

Pancho's threat must have gotten through to Lupe, for she stopped barking. But her teeth were bared, and she snarled.

"She sure is suspicious," Scurlock grumbled. "I'll make friends with her before I leave."

Pancho's face showed his doubt, but he didn't contradict his guest. He felt the coffee pot on the small cast-iron stove. "Not warm enough." he decided. "It will take only a moment to heat the coffee."

"Fine, fine," Scurlock said with false heartiness. His eyes swept the small, bare room. He would never have a better opportunity. The sheepherder's body wouldn't be found; at least, not until morning. Scurlock would be long gone by then.

He wished he could just shoot the old man and have it over, but a shot's report could carry a long way. No, it would be wisest to do this with a minimum of noise.

The dog had never stopped snarling, and Pancho

yelled at her. "Will you shut up? Go over there and lie down."

The dog sullenly obeyed him, lying down on the far side of the hut, but her teeth still showed.

"She thinks she protects me," Pancho apologized. "She can be hardheaded at times."

"Isn't this a lonely life?" Scurlock asked. He moved a step nearer to the old man. He knew what he was going to do; a knife was a silent weapon.

Lupe's head raised at this movement, and she snarled again.

Pancho glared at her, and the snarling subsided. "At times, I do not see anybody for days," Pancho agreed. "But I like it that way." He bent to pick up some sticks from the wood box beside the stove.

Scurlock drew the knife from its sheath at his belt and sprang toward Pancho. He must have made a small, scuffling sound, or some instinct alerted the old man. Pancho straightened and turned a questioning face toward Scurlock. Alarm flashed in his eyes as he saw the upraised knife, and he threw up an arm in defense.

"*Dios*," he gasped. "What is this?"

Scurlock didn't give him a chance to say more, and the arm was too late to protect Pancho. Scurlock plunged the knife into the exposed throat, driving it deep. The instant flow of blood reddened his hand, and the weight of the falling body dragged on the knife. Scurlock held onto the shaft, pulling the blade free.

He whirled at the enraged growl, and his face tightened. Lupe was on her feet, springing toward him. Scurlock wished he held a gun instead of the knife. He would have shot her regardless of the noise it might make. But there was no time to grab for the gun. He ducked and sidestepped the dog's spring, throwing out a left arm in protection against those teeth. Lupe's momentum carried her past Scurlock, but not before those wicked teeth slashed his forearm. The flooding pain ground Scurlock's teeth together.

Scurlock whirled, and the dog was coming back. All he could see were those reddened eyes and the saliva dropping from those opened jaws.

Scurlock kicked out, and his boot toe caught Lupe full on the muzzle. She yelped as the force knocked her backwards and off her feet. She whimpered as she struggled to rise, but she was dazed with pain, and her legs refused to cooperate.

Scurlock was upon her before she could get her feet under her, and a slashing stroke of the knife cut her throat.

He straightened, breathing hard, never taking his eyes off the dog. She died hard, her final convulsion lifting her body from the floor. She fell back limply and was still.

Scurlock shook from the realization of how close this had been. If he had missed that kick— He broke off the agonizing thought. He was out of this, and that was the only thing that mattered.

His forearm hurt like hell, and he cursed the wound as he looked at it. The damned bitch had slashed him deep, and Scurlock watched the blood streak down his arm. He had better do something about that in a hurry.

He leaned over, wiped off the blade on the dog's fur, then replaced the knife in its sheath. He ripped off part of the old man's shirt and bound his arm as tightly as he could. The blood slowly seeped through the cloth. At least, the bleeding was slowed.

In a sudden excess of rage, he kicked the dog's body. He was tempted to pour out the kerosene in the lamp and burn the hut down, but a fire would be a beacon that could be seen for a long way. No, it would be best to leave the hut the way it was.

Scurlock walked to the door and looked back. The room was a bloody mess, smeared by Pancho's and dog's blood. Scurlock had no doubt some of his blood was in that room, too.

His original plan called for more action, and he'd better be at it before he could leave and get attention for that throbbing arm.

He hurried out to the flimsy corral some two hundred yards from the hut. The sheep had been corralled for the night, and Scurlock heard their frightened bleating as he approached.

He tore down a large section of the flimsy poles, finding out how hampered a man could be with only one good arm.

The sheep were going crazy with fear, bunching and running around the corral. Scurlock was sweating and cursing before he pushed some of the animals through the gap. The damned, stupid things, he raved. Couldn't they see that hole? He wished to God he could shoot them down, but caution warned him against that. A fusillade of shots could too easily draw attention.

The leaders went through the wrecked fencing, and others followed them. The exertion of getting them through left Scurlock panting, and his arm felt like pure hell.

He stopped and leaned against an upright pole, waiting for the giddiness to leave him. The hard-pounding hoofs faded as the sheep vanished into the darkness. Scurlock congratulated himself on a job well done. His shooting at the woman yesterday morning and the breaking of the window were only a suggestion of what could come. If this weren't enough to convince her how unhealthy this country was, then she was a damned fool.

CHAPTER FIFTEEN

LUIS CARRIED THE SACK of salt over his shoulder as
he and Jonse walked toward Pancho's hut. The sack
was no great burden, for it was less than a third full.

"It was all I could scrape up," Luis said mournfully. "I dug out the last grain I could find."

Jonse nodded. He had watched Luis mix soot with
the salt. That should take care of the problems Pancho had mentioned.

"How long will it last, Luis?"

"Another week at best," Luis answered and
sighed.

"We'll find more someplace," Jonse said, though
he didn't know where. Even if the town had salt,
Jonse doubted anybody would sell it to him or Luis.

He watched Streak range out ahead of him. Streak
was definitely better, for he didn't move so stiffly.

Jonse laughed and said, "Maybe his new eagerness is helping him. He knows we're on the way to
see Lupe."

Luis smiled wanly. "I suspect it helps." He was in

a depressed mood this morning, and Jonse doubted that anything he could say would lift Luis's spirits.

Luis stopped as they came in sight of the hut. The sun was just rising and as yet hadn't dispelled the chilliness of the night.

"There is no smoke coming from the chimney," Luis muttered. "Pancho is already gone, or he hasn't gotten up yet."

Jonse frowned at him. Luis was in a picky mood this morning.

Streak suddenly stopped and sat down. He raised his muzzle to the sky and howled mournfully. Not you too, Jonse thought, his impatience growing. Streak was as bad as Luis. He acted as though he sensed a tragedy.

Luis shivered at the sound. "Something bad has happened," he cried.

"Oh, for God's sake," Jonse burst out. "Will you quit borrowing trouble?"

Luis dropped the sack and ran toward the hut. Jonse muttered an oath and followed him at a slower pace. Luis was determined to turn his trouble borrowing into reality.

Luis stopped in the doorway, transfixed as though shock had seized him in a giant grip.

He looked back at Jonse, and his face was ghastly, his skin so tightly drawn that he looked like a death's-head, and his eyes were blank and unseeing.

"*Dios mio*," Luis cried, his voice going higher and higher until it threatened to break. "Why do such things happen?"

An instinct warned Jonse not to let Streak go into that hut. "Get back," he said sharply. "Damn it, Streak, I mean it."

The command in Jonse's voice stopped Streak, and he sat down a dozen yards from the hut. The dog raised his muzzle and that ungodly wailing started again.

Jonse hurried on to join Luis in the doorway. "What is it?" he demanded before he looked into the hut. He was half angry over the way Luis and Streak were acting.

"Look inside," Luis said, his voice barely audible. He was close to collapsing as he leaned against the doorjamb.

Jonse looked into the hut, and his guts froze into a solid knot, making his breathing difficult. The inside of the hut looked like a slaughterhouse. At first impression, blood covered everything. Pancho lay huddled near the stove, his blank eyes staring at nothing. He had died hard, for the horror of his last few seconds was indelibly stamped on his features.

"Wait outside," Jonse brusquely ordered Luis. It was bad enough for him to go in there, it would be far worse for Luis. Streak's wailing never ceased, and the sound made Jonse grind his teeth together.

Luis appeared to be in a trance. Jonse seized his shoulder and roughly turned him. Luis's step was broken, and he moved as though he were sightless.

Jonse entered the hut and closed the door behind him so Streak couldn't follow him. He walked over to Pancho's body and stared woodenly down at it. Blackened blood was caked around the wound in Pancho's throat, and Jonse wanted to scream at the obscene cause of Pancho's death. Pancho was as harmless a man as Jonse had ever known.

Jonse forced his thoughts to appraise this gory scene. The murderer had to get close to Pancho to use a knife. That must mean that Pancho knew the man. Surely, he wouldn't have let a complete stranger into his hut.

Jonse noticed that half of Pancho's shirt had been ripped away, and Jonse puzzled over the reason.

The oppressive silence was overwhelming. If only this room could talk and tell him what had happened.

He saw another spot, three or four feet from where Pancho lay. Was this more of Pancho's blood? Jonse dispelled the question. From the wound in Pancho's throat, Jonse was sure he hadn't been able to move from the place where he fell.

He shook his head and walked over to where Lupe lay. Her teeth were bared forever in a ghastly death grimace. Whoever wielded the knife did a thorough and vicious job on her. Her head was almost severed.

Jonse studied the dog, trying to make a picture out of the meager facts before him. Had she tried to defend Pancho? Jonse nodded slowly. It was possible. He tried to visualize what had happened. Lupe must have sprung on the attacker after he stabbed Pancho. If her teeth had ripped the intruder, then the spot of blood that short distance away from where Pancho lay could be that of Pancho's attacker.

Jonse walked back to that spot and squatted down beside it. For the first time, he noticed little flecks of blood splashed about, as though somebody had shaken some injured member of his body. Jonse's eyes glowed savagely. The answers were stubborn, but they were beginning to form. The third party in this hut had torn off part of Pancho's shirt to stem a flow of blood. If that were true, Lupe's teeth had marked him well.

Jonse straightened, once more studying the room. All he had were conjectures, and he needed solid facts. He grimaced at how little he had to go on. He must look for a man with ripped flesh, with part of Pancho's shirt wrapped around the wound. Maybe he could make a beginning from that.

Jonse's face was heavy as he stepped outside and closed the door behind him.

Luis was bent over near the corner of the hut, and he was retching violently. Jonse listened to the miserable sounds and saw the convulsions of Luis's body. He suspected this wasn't the first attack.

Luis straightened and turned a ghastly face toward Jonse. He asked the first thing that came into his mind, knowing that it was a useless question. "He is dead?" he whispered.

"Yes," Jonse said roughly. Luis was too near the breaking point. The kindest thing Jonse could do for him was not to show sympathy.

"It was over quick," he said flatly. "He didn't feel a thing." He remembered Pancho's tortured features. God forgive him for the lie.

Jonse forestalled the questions trembling on Luis's lips. He didn't know who or why; at least, not yet. "He killed Lupe, too."

He saw the anguished wracking of Luis's features and said roughly, "Here now. We've got things to do."

Luis nodded and closed his eyes. He kept them closed so long that Jonse suspected he was saying a prayer.

Streak crept up close to Jonse and nuzzled his hand. He never stopped that low whining, and there was a trembling in his body.

Jonse stroked the dog's head. "I know, boy," he murmured. He recalled the first mournful wailing before they even reached the hut. Did Streak have some instinct that told him something was brutally wrong?

Jonse looked over at the holding corral. It was empty. That was to be expected. A good thirty feet of the corral's fence had been knocked down.

"We better go see if we can locate the sheep," he said in a matter-of-fact tone.

Luis stared at him with that dumb, crushed look, and Jonse thought Luis didn't hear him.

"Did you hear me?" he asked sharply.

Luis shuddered and tried to pull himself together. He tried to make a weak defense of his actions. "I cannot stop thinking about Pancho."

The roughness returned to Jonse's voice. "What the hell do you think is in *my* mind?" he said angrily. "Do we just throw up our hands and stop here?"

A degree of calmness came back to Luis, for he answered quietly enough, "No." He looked at the hut before he started away. "Do we just go away and leave him there?"

"You know better than that," Jonse said gently. "Nothing can hurt Pancho anymore. Which would be the most important right now? Spending time getting the wagon and taking Pancho back to the house, or finding the sheep?" Jonse thought he knew what Pancho would have chosen. He didn't express the paramount thought in his mind. *If we find them at all.*

Jonse and Luis separated as they set out on their search. Streak stayed with Jonse. Jonse looked at him and muttered, "I wish to God you had some sheep instinct in you. I'm afraid we're going to need help.''

Jonse scanned the ground as he walked, looking for sheep tracks, but time and the sun had restored the resiliency of the grass. He was most afraid of finding horse tracks; that would indicate riders had driven the sheep out of the corral. If that were so, Jonse thought, Luis could forget about finding his sheep. Every now and then, he looked over at Luis. Each time, Luis would shake his head. Luis had found nothing yet, either.

In a shady, damp spot, Jonse found several crushed blades of grass and the imprint of several small hoofs. He bent and fingered the edges of one of the tracks. The ground crumbled easily in his fingers. That told him that enough time had passed to dry out the hoof mark. He would say that Pancho's murder and the scattering of the sheep happened sometime early last night. He recalled how black the blood smears were. That fitted in with his estimate of elapsed time.

Jonse straightened, caught Luis's attention, and pointed at the ground. Luis started to come over, and Jonse violently waved his hands, signaling Luis to stay where he was. All he wanted was to tell Luis they were on the track of some of the sheep.

He walked along, searching for other tracks to tell him he was still headed in the right direction. Every now and then, he found a few nibbled-off blades of grass, or a hoof mark. How far would these stupid animals run? he raved.

Luis hailed him, and Jonse turned his head toward him. Luis stood on a small rise above Jonse. He pointed to his right, then beckoned Jonse to join him.

Jonse lengthened his stride, panting a little as he reached Luis. He sighed with relief as he saw what had caught Luis's attention. It wasn't all of the flock, but a considerable number of sheep were grazing ahead at Luis's right. Jonse could thank the natural instinct of sheep to bunch together instead of scattering.

They found three more bunches in another hour's searching and worked them together in a loose group. By the intent look on Luis's face, Jonse knew he was counting.

"All of them here?" Jonse asked when Luis finished.

Luis slowly shook his head. "If my count is accurate, twenty-five head are missing."

They could spend the rest of the day searching and not locate the missing sheep. The sheep could stray in later, or be forever lost. Natural predators could have had a crack at them during the night. Jonse made his decision.

"Let's work them back toward the hut." At the objection forming on Luis's face, he snapped, "Be thankful you found as many as you did. If horsemen had run them we wouldn't have found a single head." He could appreciate Luis's woe at his loss, but right now, Jonse had more important things to do than to worry over a handful of sheep.

"Damn it, Luis," he said, stopping Luis's objection. "The corral has to be repaired, if you intend to have a place to hold them tonight. You'd better stay with them. You know a hell of lot more about them than I do."

"I intended to," Luis said simply. "What do you plan to do?"

"Return to the house as fast as I can and hitch Ramon to your wagon, then take Pancho back." A thought struck him, and he asked, "Did Pancho have any relatives?"

"Only one," Luis answered slowly. "His cousin. Sixto Mejia lives in town.

Jonse nodded. "Mejia should be asked what he wants to do with Pancho's body."

"But that's not the most important thing on your mind."

"No," Jonse said savagely. He was remembering the fury that molded Andras Higuera's face as he talked to him. Andras wasn't taking any insult, real or fancied, and last night was his answer. Jonse thought that he wouldn't be going on just guesswork. Lupe had marked Pancho's killer.

"I'm going to see the Higueras again. I thought a warning was enough to make them leave you alone. It looks as though it wasn't."

"*Dios*," Luis said in a small voice, as the meaning of what Jonse said sank in. "Amigo, there are so many of them. You cannot go up against so many." Luis started to add further warning, but under Jonse's level, cold eyes, he left it unsaid. Jonse would not pay any attention to him.

Luis was unarmed, and Jonse thought of leaving him his gun, but he was certain he was going to need it.

"Luis, do you have a rifle in the house?"

"Yes, Marita will show you where it is."

Jonse sighed. Just asking for the rifle would tell Marita something was sadly wrong, but it had to be told sooner or later.

"I'll bring it back with me," Jonse said. "I'll leave

Streak with you.'' Luis was shaking his head, and Jonse said, ''At least, he can warn you. He won't allow any stranger around without barking.''

''He won't stay with me,'' Luis stated.

Jonse grinned bleakly. ''He will, if I tell him to.'' Jonse's voice sharpened. ''Streak, sit.''

Streak knew that command well. He had argued against it many times until he was convinced that resistance was useless.

His teeth bared as he drew back his lips. That was Streak's ingratiating grin, and his whine begged Jonse to reconsider.

Jonse didn't look any less stern. ''Stay,'' he said. ''I won't be gone long.''

He looked back after a dozen strides. Streak hadn't moved. Jonse lengethened his stride, thinking of how he could break this to Marita. He sighed in resignation. There was no easy way of breaking bad news.

Cribber protested Jonse's harnessing Ramon. His long shrill whinny rang out. Cribber felt good. He wanted to go.

''Maybe later today, Cribber,'' Jonse muttered.

He was hitching Ramon to the small wagon when Marita came out of the house. She was in high, good spirits, and Jonse hated to quell them.

''I heard Cribber,'' she said, ''and came out to see if something was wrong with him. Luis did not come back with you?''

''He stayed with the sheep, Marita.'' Jonse wanted to tell her about Pancho, but the words stuck in his throat.

Marita had keen perception. She looked at the wagon, then at Jonse. He had said Luis stayed with the sheep, but that was Pancho's job. "Something is wrong," she said in an unsteady voice. "Tell me what it is."

Jonse sighed. In some way, she knew that something bad had happened. Postponing telling her could only make things worse for her.

"Pancho was murdered in his hut sometime last night."

She paled, and a hand rose to her throat. "*Dios*, no," she said feebly. She swayed, and Jonse thought she would faint. He moved toward her, and she waved him away. Her breathing was still too fast, but color was returning to her face. He had forgotten how tough she was.

Tears sparkled in her eyes as she whispered, "Poor Pancho. I do not think he ever harmed anybody in his entire life."

Marita buried her face in her hands, and her shoulders shook. Jonse waited for the weakness to pass. She raised her tear-streaked face and said, "Why, Jonse? Who would do such a thing?"

It was odd that she used much the same words Luis had said. "I think both of us know the answer to that. This was only a stronger warning. Somebody is determined that you leave."

Marita dabbed savagely at the tears on her cheeks. "Never," she cried.

Jonse nodded. He knew that would be her answer. "Does Luis have a rifle in the house?" At Marita's nod, he said, "Go get it. I'm going to bring Pancho here. Then, I'll have another talk with the Higueras." His eyes smoldered. "They're hard people to convince. But this time, I'll get it through their thick heads."

She wanted to protest, and Jonse turned her toward the house. "Go," he ordered.

He finished hitching Ramon to the wagon, then searched through the shed. He was beginning to believe Luis didn't have a shovel when he found it, a thoroughly rusty tool, leaning in a corner. Jonse shook his head at its condition. It would have to do.

Jonse came out, as Marita returned with the rifle. She was frightened out of her wits, but she was still thinking, for she brought along a box of shells. Jonse took both items without comment and placed them on the wagon seat. He climbed up and lifted the reins. "I expect to be back right away."

Marita twisted her hands. "Be careful," she said.

His grin held no mirth. "I expect to be." He drove off without looking back.

He stopped before the hut. Luis and the flock were less than a half mile away, but he did not need Luis for this job.

He got the shovel out of the wagon and dug a hole large enough for Lupe. Jonse thrust the shovel into the mound of freshly turned earth and walked into the hut. Lupe wasn't heavy, but her stiffened legs made her difficult to handle. He carried her out and placed her in the hole. Jonse shoveled vigorously to work off some of the rage that kept mounting within him. Streak hadn't seen him yet, or he would be here. That was a relief. Streak's presence wouldn't make Lupe's burying any easier.

Jonse replaced the shovel in the wagon, then decided he'd better see what he could do about repairing the corral before he went in after Pancho. It took him a full half hour before he decided the flimsy corral would hold, at least for a night or two, but it needed more work. Jonse would have to leave that up to Luis, for the awareness of how time was rushing by was drawing Jonse's stomach into a hard knot. He went back to the hut and carried Pancho out to the wagon. Pancho's body wasn't much heavier than Lupe. He placed Pancho in the wagon, reentered the hut, and returned with one of Pancho's blankets. Jonse was glad when those sightless eyes were covered. He hadn't known Pancho long, but he had liked the old man.

Jonse climbed up onto the seat and drove Ramon over to the flock, stopping a short distance away to avoid frightening the sheep. Streak wanted to jump all over him, and Jonse kept saying, "Down, you jughead. Down. I told you I'd be back."

Jonse took the rifle and the shells off the wagon seat and walked over to Luis. "I've picked up Pancho," he said, "and made some minor repairs on the corral. Maybe you'll have time to rework it a little more."

Luis nodded, his eyes never leaving Jonse's grim face. "What do you do now?" he asked in a small voice.

"Why, I've got to take Ramon and the wagon back," Jonse said in mock surprise.

Luis made an impatient gesture. "You know what I mean."

"Yes," Jonse acknowledged grimly. "I'm going to see that something like this never happens again."

"You go to see the Higueras again," Luis said.

"Do you know of any better way to stop this?" Jonse asked savagely.

"But this is not your fight."

"It is now," Jonse replied. "I was here. I considered Pancho a friend of mine." He handed the rifle and shells to Luis. "I expect to be back before nightfall. If I'm not, do not let anybody into that hut unless you know who it is."

Luis's eyes were shadowed. Jonse decided the worry in them was for him and not for himself.

"I will keep the door locked," Luis promised.

"Don't go out for any reason," Jonse warned. "Even if you hear a disturbance from the sheep. Corral them, then forget them until morning." This trouble had come to a head, and Jonse wanted to impress Luis with its gravity. "I mean it, Luis," he added.

Luis nodded. He struggled with something he wanted to say, and Jonse guessed it was the same admonition he had already heard from Marita.

His hand rested briefly on Luis's shoulder. "I know what I'm doing," he said quietly. He hoped he did, but this was like diving into a pool without knowing its depth.

"I'm taking Streak with me," Jonse said. "He won't stay with you tonight. When darkness falls, he'll come looking for me."

Luis' cheeks tightened. "Amigo, I cannot tell you how much I—"

"We've been over that before," Jonse interrupted him. He softened the rebuke by saying, "There is Marita to think about. Keep your eyes open and your ears sharp."

Jonse turned and plodded toward the wagon, whistling to Streak. That was the release Streak was waiting for, and he bounded forward eagerly.

Jonse helped him up onto the wagon seat. He

didn't want Streak nosing around that blanket-covered form in the bed.

Now, another bad time was coming when Marita saw what was in the wagon. He would lose more time in consoling her before he rode into town to find Pancho's cousin. After that, he would be free to go looking for the Higueras.

CHAPTER SIXTEEN

ANDRAS HIGUERA SAT ON THE VERANDA. The morning sun was warm enough so that he should be enjoying this, but his face was moody. He had been drinking steadily since breakfast, and the decanter was almost empty. Another glass, and he would have to yell at Salvio to bring him more wine.

His thoughts were heavy and depressed. The *bien Dios* knew that something bad was rushing at the Higueras. It was more than just a feeling with Andras now. It was almost tangible enough for him to reach out and hold in his hand.

He had been in the stables last night when the *Americano* Eulalia hired had ridden in. Andras ducked into a stall. He disliked the man, avoiding contact with him whenever he could. He recognized that it could be pure jealousy, for he resented the man's standing with his mother. He saw them often with their heads together, and not once since the stranger's arrival had Eulalia taken Andras into her confidence.

His eyes glittered as he watched Scurlock put his

horse away. The man was here for no good; Andras was certain of that, but he could not speak to Eulalia about it. Whenever he tried, her eyes would burn, and her mouth would tighen into a thin line before he got out a half dozen words. Then she would order him to say no more. She threw up a barrier between them that Andras did not dare try to penetrate.

He had waited until Scurlock left the stables. The furtive air about this man drove Andras wild. The moonlight washing the stable entrance was strong enough for Andras to see the clumsy bandage wrapped about Scurlock's left forearm. Andras could not be absolutely sure, but those dark stains on the bandage could be blood. Good, he thought with a vicious enjoyment. Andras was only sorry Scurlock hadn't broken his neck.

He waited until Scurlock was gone before he left the stable. Quarreling with his man would do no good. In fact, it could hurt him, if word of it got back to Eulalia.

The incident cost him a restless night, for thinking about it would not let him sleep. He beat his hands together in futile rage. Why did Scurlock have so much influence over his mother?

Andras awakened tired and in a surly mood, and breakfast stuck in his throat. He pushed back his plate after a few bites, rose, and left the table without excusing himself. He was well aware of how Eulalia's eyes glittered at his behavior, but he was too wrought up to care much about what she thought.

How badly Andras wanted to talk to his mother about all the things that troubled him, but he could not do it while Rafael and Manuel were at the breakfast table.

Andras picked up the decanter of wine and a glass and walked outside to the veranda. The wine didn't ease his troubled thoughts. He felt as though a great storm rushed at him, and he could find no shelter.

He emptied the decanter and roared, "Salvio. Bring me more wine."

Salvio came out onto the veranda, and his face was worried. He didn't shake his head at the empty decanter, but Andras had the feeling he wanted to.

"Don Andras," he said apologetically. "Do you think it is wise to drink more? You know how the Señora disapproves."

Andras banged his fist on the table. "You dare question me?" he yelled, his face livid. His rage rose at the audacity of a mere servant daring to ask him such a question. He tried to lurch to his feet, lost his balance, and sat back down, breathing hard.

Salvio whirled and fled back into the house.

Andras glowered at the table top. *Dios*, he wished he had his quirt with him. A few licks from it would teach Salvio never to be impudent to him again.

Salvio brought the wine and stepped back from the table, well out of the reach of a blow or a kick. The tempers of the Higueras were so unpredictable.

"Can I do anything else, Don Andras?" he asked in a hushed voice.

"If there is, I'll let you know." Andras waved him away.

Andras knew what he was going to do; he was going to sit here and get gloriously drunk. That was one sure way to blot out the thoughts that plagued him.

He hadn't finished his first glass from the fresh decanter when he saw his mother and Scurlock come around the corner of the house. They stopped well out of earshot, and all his grievances rushed back in a flood. She had time to talk to that American, but she had no time for him.

Andras's eyes darkened as he watched them. Scurlock seemed to be doing most of the talking, and what he said must have pleased Eulalia, for she nodded several times. Scurlock turned to go, and Eulalia reached out and patted his arm. Scurlock turned his head and gave her a broad grin.

Seeing her pat the Americano on the arm enraged Andras more than anything else. She had three sons, but she never gave any of them such a token of approval. Andras's cheek was twitching with rage as he watched Scurlock walk away. Both of Scurlock's sleeves were pulled down and buttoned. Could Andras have imagined he saw a bandage on that left arm last night? He swore at himself for even doubting his eyes. He knew what he had seen.

Ordinarily, he would have wanted Eulalia to go on into the house without stopping to talk to him, but now he badly wanted the opportunity to speak to her.

"She will see how foolish she is," he muttered. "But then it will be too late."

Eulalia turned and saw him. She came toward him, her jaw set hard. She, too, wanted to talk.

She stopped before Andras, her eyes coldly accusing. "So now, you start drinking before the morning is fully started." She detested all males who grew so sodden with wine. The last few months before his death Bernal had been like that.

"Do you have orders against that too?" Andras asked sullenly. His wine-fed rage steadily mounted. Never could he remember receiving a compliment from her, no matter how hard he tried. But she could pat the Americano and smile at him. His jealousy and rage blended, making a powerful brew.

"Does the Americano please you?" he sneered. He pointed a finger at her. "I tell you this. He will bring you nothing but trouble. When it is too late, you will see."

She sucked in a harsh, tearing breath, and her face was pinched and ugly. "You dare talk to me like this?"

The wine gave Andras bravado. "Somebody has to," he declared.

Eulalia's face was a mask of fury, and for a moment she was speechless. She caught her breath and screamed at Andras. "Get out of my house. Do not come back until you are ready to apologize."

That scared Andras. He could feel the hollow spread in his belly. He wanted to apologize now, but he knew that if he did, he would be forever lost. He stood and looked at her with blazing eyes. "It is you who should apologize for such stupidity. Some day, you will learn."

He stalked off the veranda and turned toward the stables. *Dios*, his steps were unsteady. He was closer to being drunk than he realized. He would ride into town and finish the job of getting drunk. At least, that would keep him from thinking about this encounter.

The stable man leaped forward at Andras's appearance. "What can I do for you, Don Andras?"

"Saddle my horse, Rica," Andras ordered. He leaned against a stall partition, cutting at the wood with his quirt.

Rica didn't need to be told to hurry. One look at Andras's black face was all the encouragement Rica needed. *Dios*, Rica had never seen Andras in such a foul mood.

Andras sprang onto the saddled horse, whirled it, and with a savage slash of the quirt sent the animal racing out of the stables. Its driving hoofs sent a spray of dirt back on Rica. He crossed himself, and his hands were shaky. Something bad hovered over this hacienda. Rica could feel it, though he could not say what it was.

Andras drove his mount recklessly toward town, his face enflamed at the memory of Eulalia's words. A wave of self-pity was washing over him, and he muttered, "*Dios*, my own mother orders me out."

There had been many minor quarrels between Eulalia and Andras, but never one like this. Andras badly needed several drinks to stand between him and the encroaching fear.

The horse was breathing hard when Andras reached town. A man stepped out in front of the horse, and Andras was certain he would run him down. At the moment, he didn't care.

The man showed an amazing agility, springing back just before the horse touched him.

"Dolt," Andras screamed at him. "Look where you are going."

In that brief glimpse, Andras didn't recognize the man. He didn't give a damn who it was. Any smart man would stay out of his way today.

He pulled up before the cantina, sprang down, and lurched as he tied the reins to the hitch rack. Tomas was going to get business he hadn't expected.

CHAPTER SEVENTEEN

JONSE HAD TO ASK directions twice before he located Sixto Mejia's house. All the houses in this little town looked the same.

A slightly bent figure of a man was puttering around the yard when Jonse rode up.

"Are you Sixto Mejia?" Jonse asked.

"Sí," Mejia admitted readily. He showed no alarm, only the normal curiosity about this stranger.

Jose slowly dismounted. Mejia was younger than Pancho, maybe by ten years. Outside of the same general coloration, he could see no similarity between Mejia and Pancho, but then, they were only cousins.

"I have bad news for you," Jonse said soberly.

That brought alarm to Mejia's eyes. "What is it?"

"Pancho is dead," Jonse said bluntly.

The announcement brought sorrow to Mejia but no distress. "I could expect that," he said with simple dignity. He shrugged and spread his hands. "After all, Pancho was getting old." He squinted at Jonse. "How did you know of this?"

"Age didn't kill him," Jonse said savagely. "He was murdered sometime last night."

Mejia recoiled as though he had been struck. "*Dios mio*," he said in a shocked voice. His voice was definitely quavering. "Who would want an old man dead?"

"That's what I'm trying to find out," Jonse said grimly. "Pancho, Marita, and Luis saved my life. I've been living with them. Pancho was my friend."

Mejia looked as though his mind were empty, and he groped for something to fill the emptiness. "The last time I saw him, maybe three months ago, he seemed so content. He had nothing but praise for Marita and Luis." Mejia angrily dug a thumb joint into the corner of his eye to wipe out a tear. "Pancho and I were the last of our family," he said forlornly. "Now, there is only me."

His eyes widened as a thought occurred to him. "Are you trying to tell me Pancho and Luis quarreled?"

Jonse impatiently shood his head. "There was no quarrel. Luis and Pancho were as close as family."

Mejia sighed. "I apologize for such a thought. But who would do such a thing?" He dug at his eyes again, keeping his face averted.

"You have heard there was trouble between Señora Higuera and Marita?" Jonse asked.

"I have heard some talk of it," Mejia admitted cautiously.

Ah, he knows more than he is saying, Jonse thought, and he doesn't want to talk about it.

"*Dios*," Mejia gasped. "Are you suggesting that the Señora was responsible?"

Jonse slowly shook his head. "Not her. But I am saying that one of her sons might have done it, as a warning for Marita and Luis to get out. The day before Pancho was murdered, somebody shot out one of Marita's windows. I called Andras Higuera on it. He denied it, though the accusation made him furious. I had the feeling a guilt was behind his rage. I'm going to talk to him again. I only came into town to tell you about Pancho.''

Mejia's eyes picked up a new fire. ''The Higueras are not well liked around here, despite their great wealth. It is odd, but they seemed to have changed after Don Bernal's death. They became overbearing in their treatment of little people. People resent it, but they have too much fear of the Higueras to object too openly. Señor, you do not have to ride to the Higueras to talk to Andras. He is in town.''

Jonse leaned forward, his face intent. ''Are you sure?''

''Would I deny my own eyes?'' Mejia asked indignantly. ''I saw him less than an hour ago. He almost ran me down with his horse. He cursed me.'' Mejia smiled sourly. ''I returned his curses, making sure they were not too loud. I would bet he is still there. I watched him go into the cantina. His steps were not steady. I thought then, ho, that one is already drunk. Would a drunk leave a cantina after only a short while?'' Mejia answered his own question. ''No, he is there.''

''Where do you go?'' he demanded as Jonse turned toward Ramon.

''To talk to Andras,'' Jonse said in mild surprise. He remembered the spray of blood flecks in the hut. Lupe's teeth had marked whom ever had killed Pancho. ''I'll know when I see him if he's the one I want.''

"I go with you," Mejia said decisively. "Do not try to stop me. Don't I have the right?"

"You do," Jonse said grudgingly. He put a foot into a stirrup, and Mejia checked him. "The cantina is only block away. Is it worth riding that far?"

"No," Jonse agreed.

He walked beside Mejia, relieved that Mejia didn't try to talk. Everything that needed to be said had already been covered.

He tied Ramon beside the horse at the hitch rail before the cantina. It took only a casual glance to tell Jonse that this was the same horse Higuera rode the other morning. Mejia had saved Jonse a ride to the Higuera hacienda.

"Keep in the clear," he warned Mejia as he walked toward the cantina door. He didn't have the slightest idea of how this would go; it depended upon Higuera's temper.

Tomas's eyes were worried as he watched Andras Higuera. *Dios*, how the man was pouring down liquor. Andras was in a vile mood, complaining with every drink of how bad Tomas's liquor was, but he didn't stop drinking. Tomas thought Andras would fall down, if he didn't have the bar to cling to. Only two other customers were in the place, and they huddled together at the far end of the bar. They wanted to leave; it was in their hushed voices and apprehensive eyes, but they didn't dare walk out, for in Andras's enflamed mood, he might consider it a personal offense.

The bottle before Andras was almost empty. Tomas wanted to wring his hands with his helplessness. Should he refuse to serve Andras more liquor if he asked for it? Tomas sighed and let the thought go. He knew he didn't dare refuse such a powerful man.

"Higuera, I want to talk to you," a voice said from just inside the door. The voice jerked Tomas's head in that direction. He did not know the speaker, but Sixto Mejia followed him inside, then sidled along a wall. Mejia's actions froze the marrow in Tomas's bones. There was no mistaking what those furtive motions meant. *Dios*, *mio*, he moaned silently. There is going to be bad trouble. It is written all over the Americano's face, and Mejia's look of anticipation expressed the same thought.

"Higuera," Jonse roared. "Did you hear me?"

Higuera turned slowly, lifting his hands from the bar. It almost cost him his balance, and he swayed. He would have fallen, if he hadn't grabbed frantically for the edge of the bar.

He stared at Jonse, then shook his head in an effort to focus his eyes. "Who dares talk to me like this?" His slurred words ran together.

"You know me all right," Jonse said grimly. "I talked to you the other morning. Evidently, what I told you didn't penetrate your thick head. I warned you to leave Marita and Luis alone."

Higuera's knees kept sagging, and he kept pulling himself back up, trying hard to cling to his slipping dignity. It took tremendous effort to even recall what this fool meant.

He shrugged and said, "I do not know what you are talking about. Go away. Do not bother me any more." He started to turn back to the bar.

"Why, goddamn you," Jonse roared. "Look at me. I'm talking to you."

The room was so quiet that Jonse could hear Higuera's breathing. Down at the end of the bar, a nervous foot scuffled along the floor.

Higuera stared incredulously at Jonse, then his face turned livid. Maybe his rage let him gain a slight control of his liquor-sodden brain, for when he spoke, his words were clearer. "Sēnor," he said, biting off the title. "I do not know what you're after, but I warned you once before you cannot talk to a Higuera like this. I promise you that—"

"Shut up," Jonse said savagely. "You, or one of your brothers shot out Marita's window. But that wasn't enough to satisfy your mother. Which one of you murdered Pancho?"

Andras blinked at the enormity of the accusation. *Dios*, this made no sense at all. How hard it was to think. He looked at those blazing eyes and couldn't prevent the tiny shiver that ran through him. "I do not know what you mean," he said slowly.

"You know all right," Jonse snapped. "Which one of you three brothers did your mother send to kill Pancho? Don't try to deny it. Everybody knows how much and why she hated Marita."

Andras's eyes dilated, and his nostrils pinched together. His voice kept rising shrilly. "You insult my mother, my family."

"You worry about insults," Jonse said contemptously, "when one of you killed a harmless old man out of pure spite. Don't tell me about your mother. I heard the way she talked to Marita. She threatened to drive her out."

Andras's breathing was a rasping sound. "Do not say another word," he screamed. His back was braced against the bar, and his eyes were malevolent slits.

"I can prove whether or not it was one you, or one of your brothers," Jonse said remorselessly. He took another step toward Andras. "Pancho's dog sprang to his defense. I have every reason to believe her fangs marked him. I can see your hands but how about your forearms? Roll up your sleeves so that I can see them." Jonse's eyes never wavered. Andras was armed. How far he would go, Jonse didn't know.

Andras's face looked maniacal. "You will not touch me," he screamed.

"I'm going to look, one way or the other," Jonse said in that unyielding voice.

Andras's cheeks twitched, and he drooled at the lip corners. "Stay back," he babbled.

Jonse moved another step forward. "You can make it easy or hard on yourself," he growled.

Andras's head lifted higher, and he glared at each person in the room in turn. His face looked more set with some unknown purpose. "Do you think I would let you insult me?" Andras asked. His hand dropped to the gun at his hip.

"Look out," Mejia yelled from behind Jonse.

Jonse didn't need the warning; he had seen the motion. "Don't be a damn fool, Higuera," he cautioned.

Andras's mind was made up, and Jonse knew he couldn't change it.

Andras's movement was slow and awkward. He fought the gun, instead of drawing it out smoothly.

Jonse gave him every chance he could. He waited

until Andras's gun muzzle cleared the holster before he drew and fired. He could no longer afford to hope he could just wound Andras. The bullet slammed Andras back against the bar. He hung there a long moment, his eyes looking wonderingly at Jonse. He tried to raise the gun, but all the strength was gone from his arm. His fingers opened, and the gun fell. He grabbed with the other hand at the bar, but the same weakness was in that hand, too. A sudden wash of agony twisted his face. He doubled over and plunged forward on his face.

Jonse moved to him and toed him over, never relaxing his alertness. The precaution was unnecessary. Jonse had seen dead faces before. This one had the same slackness, as though whatever held the features together was forever gone.

The silence was a deadly chill permeating the room. Jonse's expression didn't lighten. This was the way Andras Higuera demanded it.

Jonse's eyes swept from face to face. "Every one of you saw what happened," he said harshly. "Higuera drew first."

Life returned to those frozen faces, and one of the customers laughed nervously. He cleared his throat and vigorously bobbed his head.

"Sí, señor," he said in hasty agreement. His voice was still too shrill. "He wanted to kill you."

That broke the tension in the room, and all of the watchers tried to talk at once.

Mejia came up beside Andras, and his face twisted as he looked down at the still face. "I'm glad it happened this way," he said vehemently. "He killed my cousin."

The color was just returning to Tomas's face. "All

of us saw it. What else could you do, señor? He made his choice."

Jonse nodded and dropped the gun back into its holster. He knelt beside Andras, unbuttoned the right sleeve, and rolled it up as high as he could. The forearm was unmarked.

Jonse rolled up the other sleeve. A stunned look touched his face, then he pulled himself together. Either this wasn't the one who killed Pancho, or Jonse was wrong in his assumption that Lupe's teeth had torn the killer.

He ignored the bewildered looks on the people in the room as he straightened. Jonse felt no particular remorse over his mistake, but he had no intention of talking about it. Andras Higuera was dead, but Jonse felt the major part of the responsibility was Andras's. He drew the gun that forced Jonse to kill him.

He looked at Tomas. "See that he is taken to his family." he said in a dead voice.

"Sí, señor. I will also tell them how it happened, how Andras forced—"

Jonse cut him short with an abrupt gesture. He didn't want to talk anymore about this incident.

He jerked his head toward Mejia as he passed him, and Mejia turned and followed him.

Jonse didn't speak until he got outside. He had to get back to Luis and Marita as fast as he could. At the moment, each was alone. He knew one thing. Señora Higuera wouldn't let the death of her son go unpunished. Jonse was already well aware of the scope of Eulalia's hatred. She would widen that hatred to include Jonse. That didn't arouse any particular fear in him, but the thought of Marita and Luis suffering did.

"I've got to get back to Marita Luis as fast as I can," Jonse said. "What do you want done with Pancho's body? Do you want him buried on Marita's land, or brought in here?"

Mejia lost no time in making up his mind. "Pancho hated towns, even as small as this one. No, he would want to be buried where no buildings or people crowd him."

Jonse nodded approval. "Do you want to be present for the funeral?"

"I would like to be there," Mejia said musingly. "You can go ahead. I have a horse. I will be out as soon as I can."

"I'm sorry if this gets you involved with Señora Higuera," Jonse said awkwardly.

"Don't be," Mejia said. "I have never found that very hard to do."

Jonse squeezed his shoulder a brief moment, then untied Ramon and mounted.

CHAPTER EIGHTEEN

RAFAEL PACED RESTLESSLY back and forth in the room where his mother and Manuel sat, every now and then pausing to peer out of a window. It was nearing dark, and Andras was not home yet.

"He should be here by now," he muttered. It was rare that Andras missed supper.

Eulalia cast him an annoyed look. "Let him stay away as long as he wants," she said impatiently.

Rafael's eyes were angry as he looked at his mother. Had she and Andras quarreled again this morning? He suspected they had, but when he tried to ask about it, Eulalia had almost snapped off his head.

Twice, Rafael had gone out to the stable to ask Rica if Andras had returned. Each time, Rica shook his head.

"No, Don Rafael. He has not returned." He had shaken his head to every one of Rafael's questions. "No, I do not know where he went."

Rica cast his eyes at Rafael and dared to venture a

comment. "I have never seen him in higher temper. Something drove him hard. His horse's hoofs threw sand all over me."

Rafael paced the length of the room again, his face darkening as he remembered that conversation with Rica.

"Will you sit down?" Eulalia demanded sharply.

"I cannot," Rafael replied. "Until I know that Andras is all right." Something bad was happening here. He could feel it forming all about him, though he could not see or touch it. But he could feel its cold, clammy breath, turning his spine to a long piece of ice. He wished he could read his mother's mind, but he dared not question what occupied her thoughts. At his last feeble attempt, Eulalia had screamed at him, "I know what has to be done. This is my business, you will stay out of it."

Rafael's head ached as he thought of those words. Every day, she was getting farther out of reach. That withdrawing had worried Andras too, for several times he had talked to Rafael about it. Andras had more courage than Rafael, he would try again and again to talk to his mother. Perhaps he had tried once more to reason with her. The ensuing quarrel could readily be the cause of the high temper Rica spoke of.

Rafael looked out of a window, and his body stiffened. A wagon and three riders were coming down the lane toward the house.

Eulalia caught Rafael's stiffening. "What makes you look that way?" she snapped. "Who it it?"

"Tomas driving a wagon," Rafael replied. "Three of the townspeople are with him."

"What do they want?"

Rafael cast Eulalia an injured look. How could he

answer that? He had not yet spoken to them. His shrug was expressive enough.

"It does not matter what they want," Eulalia said. "Go out and send them away."

Rafael looked at his brother. Manuel didn't shake his head, but Rafael had the impression he wanted to. Eulalia was wearing on his nerves, too.

Rafael sighed and walked to the door. Rarely did the townspeople come onto Señora Higuera's land, unless there was some urgent reason. Rafael felt that cold, clammy breath wrap around him again.

He was standing on the veranda when Tomas pulled the wagon to a stop. Rafael had never seen more distress on a man's face. His eyes swept the faces of the other three. It was odd that all three showed the same distress.

"What is it?" Rafael demanded.

None of them answered as they dismounted. Tomas climbed down from the wagon. He kept bobbing his head, and his first words were garbled.

"Speak up," Rafael said fiercely. He could feel the icy shivers racing up and down his spine.

"Please, Don Rafael," Tomas begged. "Please look into the wagon bed. We have brought him home."

Rafael glared at each of them in turn. None of them would meet his eyes.

"You fools," Rafael raged. "What are you babbling about?

He walked to the side of the wagon and looked into the bed. A form was covered with a piece of tarpaulin. Even before he reached to lift the canvas, Rafael knew. His joints seemed frozen, and his teeth chattered.

He lifted the corner of the canvas and stared into Andras's face. It was cold and immobile as stone. Rafael's tongue clove to the roof of his mouth, and he could not speak. The anguish of Andras's death was stamped on his face, and there was something else there too, a shocked wonder.

For a moment Rafael thought he was going to be violently ill. He clutched the edge of the sideboards and closed his eyes. Shutting his eyes did not blot out that monstrous sight, and shaking his head did not clear the nausea from his stomach.

He looked at Tomas and whispered, "Who did this thing?" His hands shook violently, and he shoved them into his pockets to hide them.

All four tried to talk at once, and the mounting rage swept the giddiness from Rafael's head. "Quiet," he thundered. How would he ever get the straight of this, if they all insisted upon talking at once?

Rafael pulled one hand from his pocket and stabbed a finger at Tomas. "You! Do you know?" At Tomas's frightened nod, Rafael said, "Then tell me."

"It was the Americano," Tomas said in a voice that shook so badly he could barely form the words.

"What Americano?" Rafael demanded.

"The one who lives with Marita and Luis. I had not heard of him before, but apparently, Marita has hired him." Tomas shivered under the merciless raking of Rafael's eyes.

"Go on." The quietness in Rafael's voice fooled no one. It did not hide the deadliness in his tone.

"They had some kind of quarrel," Tomas rushed on. "I do not know what it was about. Don Andras had been drinking very hard. He was drunk when the Americano walked in. Sixto Mejia was with him. The

Americano told Don Andras that Pancho, Luis's shepherd had been killed.''

Rafael's eyes narrowed. "Did this American accuse my brother of the killing?"

Tomas's eyes begged for understanding. "I saw there was going to be bad trouble. I backed away as far as I could get. I do not know whether or not he accused Don Andras. But whatever he said seemed to make Don Andras go crazy. He screamed that no one could insult him in that manner." Tomas paused to draw a deep breath. "Then Don Andras tried to draw his pistol. The Americano yelled at him to stop, but Don Andras was beyond reason."

"Then the American killed my brother," Rafael hissed.

"Sí," Tomas said sadly. "He was very fast with a gun."

"You liar," Rafael said viciously. "You are saying my brother was responsible for his own death."

Tomas was frightened, but he stood his ground. "It happened exactly as I have described it. Gomez and Villa were there, too. They saw it the same way."

Villa and Gomez nodded reluctantly. They were as frightened as Tomas.

"Liars," Rafael screamed. "Every one of you." He wished he had his gun. He would kill all of them.

They shrank back before his rage. They were badly scared but not enough to change their story. "It is true," Tomas said stubbornly. "Sixto Mejia was there. He saw it the same way."

Rafael glared at him. His mind a churning mass of tormented grief. Andras was his beloved brother. Rafael wanted to rush at Tomas and beat the lying words out of him with his fists, then a saner portion of his mind told him Tomas and the others were not lying. They were simple men; too simple to make up an elaborate story. They only told it the way it happened.

"Wait here," he said in a voice as brittle as thin ice. "The Señora must be told about this."

Rafael turned and walked into the house. He entered the room where Eulalia and Manuel sat, and something in his face told them he carried bad news, for their faces went tight with strain.

"What is it?" Eulalia cried. "Why are they here?"

"They brought Andras home," Rafael said dully.

"Was he so drunk that he could not sit his horse?" she asked contemptuously.

"Do not say such things about him," Rafael flared in brief rebellion. The rebellion was gone quickly, and the dullness returned. "Andras is dead. He is in the wagon."

Manuel sprang to his feet, his face twisted with disbelief. "There must be a mistake," he cried.

Rafael shook his head. There was no mistake. His eyes never left Eulalia. He expected her face to collapse in the ruin of grief, but she surprised him. Her face went tight and pinched, and she sucked in a deep, shuddering breath. She briefly closed her eyes, but when she reopened them, there were no tears.

She stood, and Rafael thought she swayed slightly. "Take me to him," she said.

Ah, Rafael thought, the grief is deep within her. He should have known his mother would hide it well.

Rafael led Eulalia and Manuel out to the wagon. The three townspeople jerked their hats off and withdrew a few paces at her approach.

"Señora," Tomas said haltingly. "I am so sorry."

She swept him with those cold eyes. "Does Don Rafael know all about this?"

Tomas looked at the ground as he answered. "We told him everything that happened." His lips moved as though he sought further words, and she stopped him.

"Don Rafael will tell me about it," she said.

Rafael lifted the canvas for her to look at Andras's face. He expected her to break then. This time he was certain she swayed. To Rafael it seemed as though she stared for an eternity at Andras before she said, "Take him inside."

The townspeople sprang to obey her, and she waved them aside. "My sons will take care of it," she said curtly.

Rafael and Manuel carried Andras inside and laid him on the bed in his bedroom.

Eulalia sat down beside the bed. "How did it happen?" she asked quietly.

Rafael told her everything he heard from Tomas and the other. "They said the American was big," he finished.

"So Marita has hired an American," Eulalia mused, and her face was ugly. "That will be taken care of."

The rebellion was a lashing force within Rafael, but he gave it no voice. He supposed she would ask the redheaded Americano to take care of Marita's new help. Rafael would not allow that. He was going to take care of it, himself. He did not intend to argue with his mother about it. He would merely leave sometime during the night.

Eulalia stared at Andras again. "We will bury him

in the morning," she said in a voice barely audible. "Now, leave me."

Rafael looked back from the door of the room. Eulalia stared fixedly at the face of her oldest son. Rafael doubted that she knew he and Manuel were alive right now.

"Should she be left alone like that?" Manuel asked uncertainly.

"You go tell her that," Rafael said sourly.

Manuel's hands bunched, and his voice was filled with passion. "The goddamned Americans," he said in a shaking voice. "Everywhere they go, they cause trouble."

"Do not worry about it," Rafael said harshly. "I'm going to change that."

CHAPTER NINETEEN

SIXTO MEJIA CHOSE THE spot for Pancho's burial. He stopped in the shade of a tree some two hundred yards from the hut. He looked at Marita and Luis and asked, "Would this be all right?" Pancho would be close to his sheep and the place he called home. "This would please him."

Luis nodded. For an instant, Marita lost her composure, then she managed to control her emotions. "You have chosen well, Sixto," she said calmly.

Jonse helped dig the grave, then lent a hand in lowering the blanket-wrapped form. None of the three said a word after the grave was filled. They stood with stolid faces. Jonse knew that every thought was for Pancho's eternal rest and contentment. This tribute suited Jonse. A thought was an honest thing. Words could be too easily twisted and distorted, mocking the true meaning behind them.

Mejia shook his head sadly and said, "I will carve him a suitable headstone." He glanced questioningly at Marita. "If I am allowed to stay here long enough."

"You are welcome to stay as long as you wish," Marita said.

"I am glad to hear you say that," Mejia replied. "I would like to stay much longer. I would like to take Pancho's place. You would not be hiring a man who knows nothing about sheep. I was a herder in my younger years." He saw the frowns forming on Marita's and Luis's faces and looked anxiously from one to the other.

If they hired Mejia, it would solve a tough problem for Jonse. Jonse could not stay with Marita and Luis at the same time, and he had an icy feeling that both of them should be guarded.

"Why, sure," Jonse said. "You know we need a man."

The frown increased on Marita's face. "Ordinarily, I would say yes quickly. But what will the Higueras do about Andras's death? Even when I think about that, my throat tightens. I could not allow Sixto to run the risk."

"Pancho was my cousin," Mejia said stubbornly. "The last of my family. I think you should give me the privilege of countering whatever they might do."

Luis nodded reluctantly as though he were swinging Jonse's way, but Marita looked as unyielding as ever. "I could not let him risk his life," she said passionately. "Who knows what she will do next?"

That was a question Jonse couldn't answer, but Marita had to look at this from another angle. "Hiring Mejia means that Luis wouldn't spend the night out here alone," Jonse pointed out. "Do you expect Luis to stay awake all night? If Sixto was with him, Luis could get a few hours sleep."

Marita's eyes were startled. "You would not stay with him?"

"Who stays with you?" Jonse asked with brutal candor. "I think Andras's death will drive the Señora into a direct attack. Where would that attack be likely to come?" Jonse answered his own question. "On the house. Do you want to be there alone?"

The familiar strain was back in Marita's face, and Jonse was afraid she sould cry. *"Madre de Dios,"* she said. "Will it never end?"

Jonse grinned at her, trying to lighten her mood. "Everything does, if you can wait long enough."

That brought a wan smile from Marita. "I am afraid my waiting has just about run out."

Jonse felt much the same way. All he wanted right now was to get through the night without harm to any of them. With daylight, he could plan ahead. Right now, he was too damned tired to do much thinking.

Marita and Jonse sat in the dark and talked for a long time. Marita started to light a lamp, and Jonse said, "No lights, Marita. If they come, we don't want to make things easier for them."

"I'm frightened, Jonse," she confessed.

"Two of us," Jonse said gruffly. It was never pleasant to think of being a target without even knowing from which direction the attack would come. If Señora Higuera marshaled every man she had, there was no possible way of stopping them. Jonse shrugged. It was no use beating his brains out when nothing had yet happened.

"Marita," he said. "Go get some sleep.

"How could I sleep at such a time?" she protested.

"It might let me get a little sleep," Jonse said practically.

She laughed, a little burst of sound with no mirth in it. "You will not sleep," she said. "I know you. But I will give you your chance. Good night, Jonse."

"'Night," he responded absently. She would sleep; as tired as she was, she could not help it. Jonse might doze off a little, his tired body would see to that.

He waited until he was sure Marita had closed her eyes. He slipped out of the house, easing through the partially opened door as fast as he could, only breathing fully when the door was closed behind him.

The night was too still. He stood there a long moment, listening. He thought the usual night sounds were missing, but that could be a product of an overwrought imagination. He hadn't been thinking very clearly. He had a good sentry, and he wasn't using him.

He hurried to the shed and let Streak out. Streak barked his joy, and Jonse quieted him. "This is no playtime, boy," he said.

Streak sensed something was amiss, for his barking stopped. He followed Jonse to the house, and Jonse stopped him at the door. "You stay out here, Streak. You listen real good. You hear me?"

Streak wriggled under Jonse's patting, but he made no sound.

Jonse felt better after he reentered the house. A dog had keener senses than any man. If Jonse dozed off now and then, he wouldn't jerk awake with a guilty feeling. Streak was out there. He would raise hell if anybody tried to approach.

Jonse sat down in a chair and leaned his rifle against it. Quiet, he thought fretfully; too damned quiet. Why was he torturing himself so? Streak was out there to give him advance warning. Lupe had been with Pancho too, he thought ironically. She hadn't done Pancho much good.

His eyelids grew heavier and heavier. Fighting sleep only intensified its stealthy attack, making it irresistible.

"Not going to sleep," Jonse muttered. "Got to—"

That was the last he remembered. He awakened with a start, feeling guilty. It was still dark; at least he hadn't slept the night through. He rolled his shoulders to ease the ache in them, and grimaced as he stood. Something had thrust needles all through his legs.

He walked a dozen steps, and the needles went away. Jonse shook his head at his own weakness. Well, sleep was about the best way he knew of to spend some anxious time.

He crossed to a window and looked to the east. Hell, you slept a long time, he muttered. That light band of gray in the east meant the approach of dawn; real or false he didn't know. Damned, if he wouldn't give half of his soul for a cup of coffee.

He thought he was being particularly quiet, but he must have awakened Marita, for she appeared in the doorway of her bedroom.

"I'm sorry I woke you up," he apologized.

She shook her head in quick denial. "I have been awake for a long time, then I heard you stirring around. You didn't get any sleep," she said contritely.

Again, Jonse felt that guilty stab. He'd probably slept more than she had. "I dozed off," he lied. "Marita, I'd give my soul to the devil for a cup of coffee." He made the offer even more attractive than when he first thought of it.

She shook her head in reproof at his blasphemy but asked, "Is everything all right?"

"It's been quiet," he assured her. He wished he could promise that it was going to continue that way, but he couldn't.

Jonse walked to a window and looked out to the east again. The band of gray was getting a rosy tint to it. That was the real dawn he had seen.

He heard Marita putting wood into the stove and knew that a thin plume of smoke would arise from the chimney, making a beacon that could be seen for a long way.

Damn it, he thought angrily. They couldn't cower like two frightened, trapped rats; they had to go on living.

The good smell of coffee filled his nostrils, and his stomach rumbled. A damned stomach went on living regardless of the situation.

He drank two cups, savoring every swallow. He shook his head at Marita's proffer of a third cup.

"This will hold me," he said. "I want to go out and look around." He saw the harried look in Marita's eyes and the drawn hollow look that came into her face. "Here now," he admonished. "I'm not going far."

He picked up his rifle and opened the door. His eyes swept about him. He couldn't see anything that was alarming. It was going to be a brilliant day. A man couldn't pick a better day to die, he thought with macabre humor.

Jonse took a step away from the door, and Streak jumped all over him. With his free hand, Jonse pushed him back to the ground. "Ole nuisance," he said affectionately. He knew Streak hadn't moved away from the door all night.

Jonse bent to pet him. That movement saved his life. The evil, humming passage of a rifle bullet sounded just over his head. He didn't let startled reaction freeze him. He dove for the ground and wriggled toward the door. Whoever was doing that shooting had a hasty trigger finger, for two more slugs slammed into the door before Jonse reached it.

Marita must have raced toward the door the moment she heard the first shot, for the door was flung open in Jonse's face. He was grateful for that. It saved him the loss of precious seconds in straightening and reaching for the knob.

"Streak," he snapped. "In here." For the first time, Streak was allowed in the house. The dog bounded forward, and Marita slammed the door behind him.

"Get down," Jonse yelled at Marita and wiped his forehead. He wasn't surprised to find his fingers damp.

"Looks like somebody's mad at me," he said in a wry attempt at humor.

Marita dropped to her hands and knees. "They could have killed you," she whispered.

Jonse motioned her over to the base of a wall. He could agree with what she said, but he wasn't going to worry about something that hadn't happened. Marita could be wrong when she said "they." Jonse thought there was only man out there.

The ambusher must be in an excess of rage, for he shot out all of the windows on that side of the house.

Jonse crawled to a window and peered out of the lower corner. He grunted with satisfaction as he saw a puff of smoke lift lazily from the small rise some two hundred yards from the house. That marked the location of the rifleman for him.

"Looks like only one," he said.

Jonse almost knew satisfaction as two more shots ripped through a window. It looked as though the ambusher's rage at his failure was keeping him here. Jonse hoped so; he wanted the expectation of him coming out through that door again to hold the rifleman in place.

"Got to do something about this," he said and crawled toward the rear door. "Get back, Streak," he ordered as the dog started to follow him. "You stay with Marita."

Streak whined his protest, but he stopped.

"You cannot go out there," Marita cried.

Jonse impatiently shook his head. If she was thinking rationally, she would know there was nothing else he could do.

"I know what I'm doing," he said calmly.

He crawled up to the rear door, reached for the knob, and opened the door only wide enough for him to pass through. His skin was tight as he slipped out of the partially opened door. This was the big gamble; he didn't know whether or not another man waited for him outside that door.

CHAPTER TWENTY

RAFAEL THOUGHT DAWN would never come. *Dios*, he had been lying here for so long that his bones were getting stiff. Not once had he taken his eyes off the door of that house. Sooner or later, the American had to come out. He shifted restlessly to relieve his aching muscles. His mother had no idea of where he was; Rafael doubted she even knew he was gone from the hacienda. If things went as he anticipated, he should be back before breakfast time. He hoped so. It would be sacrilege to miss Andras's funeral.

The light strengthened, and he saw the dog walking back and forth before the door. Rafael wasn't interested in the animal. He wanted to see a man come out.

He sucked in a rasping breath as the door opened, and snugged the rifle butt to his shoulder. At this distance he should not miss.

A man stepped out of the door. Rafael's eyes glittered with rage. There was no doubt this was the Americano. His size alone made him outstanding.

The dog leaped on the man and was pushed back to the ground. Rafael would never have a better shot. He squeezed the trigger just as the man bent to pat the dog. Rafael didn't have to see where the bullet hit to know he had missed. He sobbed with rage as he fired twice more at the figure. *Dios*, that one could move in a hurry. He was on the ground before Rafael could adjust his sights, and Rafael swore he could crawl faster than a snake. The man wriggled inside the door, and the dog followed. The door slammed shut.

Rafael wanted to scream out his frustrated rage. He shot out every window he could see, then a degree of sanity returned to him. He had plenty of ammunition with him, but this was a senseless waste. He settled down for a long wait. The Americano would come out again. Then he would learn how endless Rafael Higuera's patience was.

Jonse straightened up against the back wall of the house and blew out a weak sigh of relief. Nobody had fired at him. Now he was almost positive he had only to deal with the one in front of the house. But how to get at him? Jonse spat on the ground as he pondered. It would take a long, circuitous route to approach the man from the rear. He had to use extreme caution to avoid being seen. He sure as hell didn't want rifle bullets peppering anywhere around him.

Jonse nodded as he made his decision. "Here goes," he muttered, drew a deep breath, then darted from the house to the wagon some fifty yards away. He prayed that the ambusher's attention was riveted solely to the front door of the house.

Jonse replenished the air in his lungs, then dashed

for the shed, any moment expecting a bullet to nip at his heels. That was one hell of an amateur out there, or he was so eaten up with hatred, that he wasn't thinking or seeing very clearly. Or he's gone, Jonse thought in dismay.

He shook his head impatiently at the thought. He didn't want that. If possible, he wanted to talk to the man; at second choice, he would gladly shoot him.

Jonse's way was a lot easier now. He used the shed for cover, and when he reached its end, he was farther away from the rise where he had noticed the smoke. But he expected that. He was going to cover quite a bit of ground to get behind the ambusher. Jonse didn't mind that, but he deplored the time it was taking. Already, it seemed as though he had been stalking the man for an eternity.

Jonse reached the end of the shed and weighed his course. A dozen yards away, a small wash started. It led farther away from the rise, but it offered additional protection.

Jonse dropped to his hands and knees and crawled into the depression. He blew out an explosive breath of relief as the short banks rose on each side of him. Maybe he was only fooling himself, maybe the man on the rise could see into the depression, but Jonse felt as though he were hidden.

He crawled until he thought his elbows and knees were wearing thin. It felt as though he had crawled a mile when he finally decided it was safe to rise from the wash.

Jonse peered over the edge. He had crawled quite a way, for the ambusher's rise was quite a way behind and to his left. Now, he could cut an angle and come in behind the rise.

He snaked over the lip of the wash but didn't dare stand until he reached a few scrubby trees. A flitting shadow moved from tree to tree. Jonse's sense of security strengthened each time he made a little progress, but it was taking too long.

Every now and then, he evaluated the rise's location. He was well behind it now; it should be safe enough to cut straight toward it.

Fear was still with Jonse, but it came from a different source. He was afraid he had taken too much time, the ambusher would be long gone by now.

He sank down to the ground as he saw a horse tethered to his right. Jesus, he thought, he's still here. That one's hatred must be strong to keep him anchored so long.

Jonse avoided going near the horse. It was aware of him, for its head was turned toward him, watching his every move. But it made no sound, and that was the important thing.

Jonse reached the upward tilt of the rise and dropped to the ground. He had more of that damned crawling ahead of him, and his prone position would cut severely into his field of vision.

He used every tuft of grass, every bush, to conceal his progress. Surely, he must be near the top, but he hadn't seen a damned thing. Then a flash of movement caught his eye, not fifty yards ahead of him. The color in the movement marked the man's position for Jonse. A savage sense of satisfaction seized him. This one was a fool to stay here so long.

Jonse got slowly to his feet. Now, he could see the figure on the ground. He took a cautious step, then another. This should be more than close enough. He put the rifle butt against his shoulder and said in a loud voice, "You! Stand up. And leave that rifle on the ground."

That must have been a horrible shock to the man, for Jonse saw the startled jerk that ran through the figure. If he heard the warning, it meant nothing to him, for he whirled around and frantically scrambled to his knees. His face was contorted as he tried to swing his rifle muzzle around.

This man was a damned fool to try something like that with rifle sights trained on him. Jonse fired before the ambusher's rifle completed its arc.

The man reared up, almost making it to his feet. He flung his arms wide, throwing the rifle from him, before he collapsed to the ground.

Jonse watched hard-eyed for the slightest movement from the crumpled figure. He didn't regret shooting the man, but he did wish he had had a chance to question him. That was a futile wish now.

He advanced cautiously, his rifle ready. He toed the figure over and stared down into a face he had never seen before. Jonse noted the richness of his dress. It was a safe guess that this was one of the Higueras.

Jonse's eyes widened as he saw the faint fluttering of the lips. This one wasn't dead, but by the shallow breathing and the waxy color of his face, he was close to it.

Jonse bent down and listened to the reedy breathing. The massive stain on the man's right shoulder marked where Jonse's bullet hit. This man was hit hard and losing blood fast. Jonse better do something and soon, or that reedy breathing would snap off.

He found a handkerchief in one of the man's

pockets, wadded it, and placed it against the wound. His own handkerchief was just long enough to bind the wad to place. That was all he could do now.

The man carried no other weapon, and Jonse walked over to the rifle, picked it up by the barrel, and hurled it farther away. He didn't think the wounded man would get up on his own, but he was taking no chances. He turned and went down the slope in long, hurried strides.

The horse's eyes rolled, and he snorted nervously at Jonse's approach, but that was the limit of his fight. That was a big relief, Jonse thought, as he untied the reins. This could be one of the wild ones, putting up a vicious resistence against a stranger.

Jonse led him up the hill, stopping the animal beside the wounded man. The smell of blood increased the horse's nervousness, and it kept dancing and whirling as Jonse tried to lift and load the body. Jonse kept up soothing words, though he wanted to swear at the animal. The horse finally quieted enough for Jonse to lift the body and lay it across the saddle. It was a damned good thing the man wasn't any heavier.

Jonse looked dubiously at the dangling weight before he started. All he could do was pray that the man didn't slip off to one side or the other.

He went down the hill toward the house, leading the horse slowly.

Marita had seen him coming, for she was waiting outside the house when Jonse arrived.

"I heard the shot," she said, a remnant of the dread in her eyes. "I thought it could be—" She briefly closed her eyes and didn't finish. She looked at the man and asked in a small voice, "Is he dead?"

"Damned near it," Jonse answered. "Is it all right to take him inside?"

"Oh yes," she breathed.

Jonse lifted the man from the saddle and carried him into the house.

Marita handed him a knife, and Jonse slashed away the jacket and shirt. The wound was an ugly one, its ingress showing an angry, inflamed purple.

"Looks like it went clear through," Jonse said. "But it shattered some bones. He'll have little use of that arm again." If he lives, he finished mentally.

Marita washed the wound, applied some salve to it, then bound it tightly. "I can do no more," she said helplessly.

"Nobody could have," Jonse assured her. Her hands trembled a little, but she was calm. That spiritual toughness was showing again.

Jonse looked down at the motionless face. Some color was beginning to steal through it. "Do you know him?"

Marita nodded mutely, then her words rushed out in a torrent. "Rafael Higuera. Eulalia's middle son."

"She hates real good, doesn't she?" Jonse said drily.

"Are you going to take him back to her?" Marita asked in a hushed voice.

Jonse shook his head. "He couldn't stand much more moving right now. I'm hoping he'll regain consciousness. I'd like a few answers."

That was the longest fifteen minutes Jonse ever spent. The color in Rafael's face grew stronger, and he moaned softly. Then his eyes opened, and he stared dazedly up at Jonse.

A blaze started in his eyes, sweeping away the pain. "The Americano," he said hoarsely. "You killed my brother." He sobbed, and a cough broke up the sound. "*Dios*, I wanted so badly to kill you."

"You tried," Jonse said matter-of-factly. "Shut up," he said harshly as Rafael tried to speak again. "I didn't want to kill your brother. He forced me." His face was earnest as he leaned closer to Rafael. "All I wanted to do was to see his hands and forearms. I believe Pancho's dog tore whoever killed Pancho. Andras refused to let me see them. He yelled something about me insulting him, then drew." Jonse's face hardened. "Why would your mother want a harmless old man killed?"

Rafael's eyes wide with shock, and for a moment, Jonse was afraid it was reaction to his wound.

Rafael feebly shook his head. "No, no," he denied. "She had nothing to do with it. It had to be the Americano she has been letting stay around. Yesterday, I saw a bandage on his left forearm. When I asked him about it, he told me to mind my own business."

"Ah," Jonse said as he straightened. Here was his answer. Rafael might not blame his mother, but Jonse did. She had hired an American to drive Marita and Luis out. It had cost her a terrible price; first Andras and now Rafael.

Rafael tried to say something, but his eyes were closing.

Jonse listened a moment, then said, "He's sleeping. He needs it."

Marita read something in Jonse's face, and she asked, "Where do you go now?"

He looked at her mild surprise. She should know

the answer to that. "Why, I'm going to stop this once and for all. I'll ride out and get Luis. I want him to stay with you."

Marita was going to say something more, and Jonse shook his head at her. She should know him well enough by now to know he wasn't a reckless man.

She smiled faintly, as she touched his arm. "I know, Jonse. I won't say it. *Vaya con Dios*."

Jonse gave her brief smile as he walked toward the door.

CHAPTER TWENTY-ONE

EULALIA HIGUERA WAITED impatiently for Manuel to return to the house. A cold ball of fear lay like a stone in the pit of her stomach. Rafael was not in the house, so she had sent Manuel to the stables to ask Rica if he had seen him.

Manuel came into the room, shaking his head. "Rica has not seen him. But Rafael's horse is not there. Rica has no idea of when Rafael took him." He stared at Eulalia, an unknown fear beginning to gnaw at him.

The cold ball of fear had grown in weight in Eulalia's stomach and was beginning to hurt. She thought she knew where Rafael had gone; he had gone to kill the Americano at Marita's. She felt like wringing her hands, but that would be a weakness she would not display before Manuel.

She kept her face carefully blank, though torment was tearing her apart inside. *Dios mio*, she prayed. Do not let anything happen to Rafael. I saw the hatred in his eyes each time we spoke of the

Americano who killed Andras. I told Rafael it would be taken care of, but no, he would not listen to me. Though he did not say so, it was something he had to do himself. Protect him, *Dios*. Protect him.

Her legs shook, and she felt as though she were crumbling inwardly, breaking off a small piece at a time until soon only a hollow shell would be left. Andras was not yet buried, and here Rafael was gone. She chewed savagely on her lower lip to keep the welling screams from tearing her lips apart.

Nothing showed on her face when she faced Manuel again. "Manuel, go find Scurlock. Tell him I want to see him now."

Manuel couldn't keep his distaste for Scurlock out of his eyes. He had talked over with his two brothers why his mother should hire this man, but none of them came up with a plausible solution. Now, his mother was calling on the American again.

"Madre," he said hesitantly. "I could do anything he can—"

"Stop it," she shrilled. It was effort to bring her voice back to normal. "Do as I say," she ordered. "I know what I am doing."

Manuel tried to meet her eyes and couldn't. He turned and walked out of the room.

Eulalia paced the room while she waited for Scurlock. She knew that yesterday Scurlock had done nothing about what he was hired to do. He had stayed around the house all day, making excuses about his injured arm. He even lifted his sleeve so that she could see the bandage. His explanation was that his fool horse had carried him through low-hanging tree branches, and the branches had scraped him.

Eulalia looked at her tightly clenched hands. Was

she breaking up? she wondered. She forced her hands open and put her mind solely on what had to be done. Today, she would accept no excuses from Scurlock. He either accomplished what she demanded, or she would order him to get out.

She moved a few more steps, realizing how weak that reasoning was. If she ordered him out, who would she send against the American Marita hired? That wicked gleam appeared in her eyes as she thought she knew best how to handle Scurlock. She would offer him double the price she orginally set. That should take care of any of Scurlock's objections.

She resumed that agitated pacing. *Dios*, would the fool never come?

Scurlock came into the room, that ingratiating smile on his lips. It faded quickly as he saw Eulalia's expression. He shouldn't have come in here grinning, not after what happened yesterday.

"Sēnora," he said smoothly. "I didn't get a chance to tell you, but I'm powerful sorry to hear about Andras."

Eulalia's face didn't change, and Scurlock thought, She's made of ice, and nothing's going to change her.

"Did you hear who killed Andras?" she demanded.

"No, I didn't," Scurlock confessed. "If you know who it is, I can go after him."

Some of the awful bleakness left her face. "*Dios*, how I hoped you would say that. He is an Americano, hired by Marita."

Scurlock's pulses jerked and twanged, and he felt nausea growing in his stomach. "Who is this American? Have you seen him?"

Eulalia made an impatient gesture. She could not see how these questions were important. "I do not know his name," she said irritably. "Yes, he is a very big man. He killed Andras. I want him killed. I will pay you a thousand dollars more for just this job. After it is done, you can then run out Marita and Luis."

Scurlock's throat started closing on him. Hell, it couldn't be; this was only coincidence, but the man who had chased him so relentlessly had been a big man, too. Scurlock felt the sweat coming out on his forehead, and the moisture was cold. The proffer of the additional money made Scurlock's head swim. Good God, that would be two thousand dollars. He would have more money at one time than he had ever had in his life, or ever hoped to have. His sweating increased. What if this was the same man who had chased him all through those terror-filled weeks? That one had been big, too. Oh, God, if he only had a name, or a general description other than just big, then he would know if it was the same one. He argued with himself, pointing out how impossible that could be. He had shaken off his pursuer, or he would have heard of him before now. The percentage was all against the probability that the man Señora Higuera wanted killed and the one who chased him could be the same. But the growing lump of fear in his belly warned him he couldn't take the smallest chance. The Señora couldn't offer him enough money to have that merciless tracker on his trail again.

Scurlock's thoughts were running wild, and he fought to control them. The smartest thing he could do was to get out of this country as fast as he could. Avarice wouldn't let go its clutch on him. Even if he left now, he might be able to turn this to some advantage.

Scurlock's eyes shone with cupidity. "I can do it," he said slowly. The lie rolled easily off his lips. "But I'll need some advance money." He held his breath as he waited for her reaction. From experience, he knew how tight her hand was on the purse strings.

"How much?" Eulalia asked coldly.

Those damned eyes were burning into him again. Scurlock tried to think of a figure she would accept. If he made it too big, she would refuse. If he made it less than she might give him— He groaned at the thought of how much he could lose in this transaction.

"A hundred dollars," he said boldly. He had most of the fifty dollars she had already given him. That plus an additional hundred would carry him a long way.

Eulalia stared at him with that odd glitter in her eyes, and Scurlock died as he waited for her to speak. Then, she nodded abruptly, turned, and left the room.

I could have gotten more, he mourned. He wanted to call her back and raise the sum, but he knew that wouldn't be wise; not with her temper.

She came back and dropped five twenty-dollar gold pieces into his palm. "The rest of it when he is dead," she said passionately. "I want him killed before the sun sets."

"Sure," he answered. He thought sardonically, By the time the sun sets, I'll be a long way from here. You fry your own fish, Señora Higuera. Scurlock's stride lengthened after he left the house as he headed for the stable. The coins tinkled pleasantly in his pant pockets. The sound of them didn't make him regret a thing. He might have gotten more, but he had never been a wishy-washy man. Once he made a decision, he stuck to it. It was odd that the hard little knot of fear still remained in his belly. He had the instincts of an animal, and this one told him to get out of here as fast as he could.

"*Buenos dias, Señor,*" Rica greeted him.

Scrulock waved him quiet. He didn't have time to waste on pleasantries. "I'm in a hurry, Rica," he growled. "Saddle my horse."

Rica's face turned blank. "Si," he said and hurried toward a stall.

CHAPTER TWENTY-TWO

JONSE RODE DOWN the long lane to the Higuera hacienda and entered the courtyard. He didn't know what he would find here, but the leaders in his neck were too tight, telling him it could only be trouble. He pulled up at the edge of the veranda and sat motionless a long moment. If anyone saw him coming, they weren't coming out to offer him any invitation.

He shook his head as he dismounted. It didn't matter. With an invitation or not, he was going to look through this house. Rafael told him that an American with a bandaged arm was staying here. Jonse was sure he was telling the truth. A man hurting as badly as Rafael rarely found the strength to fashion lies.

Jonse stepped up onto the veranda and loosened the pistol in his holster. He didn't know what he would find in here, but he could be certain it wouldn't be pleasant.

He raised a hand to knock on the door when the sound of hoofs coming that way stopped his motion.

Ah, he thought, somebody was around, and they were coming to investigate why he was here. He stepped off the vernada just as a rider turned the corner of the house, not fifty feet away.

In just a glimpse, Jonse caught the white of a bandage on the man's left forearm, and the rider was American. It was more than enough. Finding this one wasn't nearly as difficult as Jonse anticipated.

"I want to talk to you," Jonse roared.

A frozen, startled grimace molded the rider's face, and his reaction was violent and unexpected. He dug in his spurs and grabbed for the gun at his hip. The horse leaped forward in a long bound under the torment of the spurs and was gaining speed with the second bound.

Jonse drew his gun, but this had broken too quickly and he was slower than the rider. A flash of sunlight reflected from the gun in the rider's hand as the weapon was pointed at Jonse. Jonse felt tense and awkward as his hand holding the gun rose. It was a certainty he wasn't going to get the first shot. But one thing was in his favor. Shooting from the back of a running horse made a target hard to hit, even one man-sized.

A bullet hummed by Jonse's head, and he ducked involuntarily. He heard the heavy, flat report of the second shot, but this one wasn't as close as the first, for Jonse didn't hear its passage. He held his fire until the horse was opposite him, taking the easier angle of a broadside shot rather than the more difficult head-on target.

He pulled the trigger and grunted with wicked satisfaction. The rider flung up his arms, letting go of the reins and his gun. He was all loose in the saddle, but he managed to stay erect for another jump. Jonse fired again. The rider collapsed all at once, plunging heavily to one side. His boot caught in the stirrup and held for two more running strides before it worked free. He slid along the ground with the momentum, then crumpled up.

Jonse warily approached him. He knew this man was hard hit, but he took no chances, ready to shoot again at the slightest movement.

Jonse stood over him, his eyes going wide in shock as he saw the red hair and the prominent scar on the man's face. Rage shook him, and he was tempted to empty the pistol into the body. This was the one who killed Marcia, the one he had trailed so long. Jonse's head was filled with a roaring, and he was momentarily blinded. Then sanity slowly returned to him, clearing his head and vision. There was no sense in shooting a dead man.

But he was wrong. He almost fired again as he saw the eyes slowly open.

The man stared foggily up at Jonse, then comprehension returned to his eyes. It gave Jonse a weak sense of satisfaction. This man knew him.

The man coughed weakly, sending out a spray of bloody flecks. The coughing wracked him, and the stain on his chest grew rapidly.

"I guess I always knew you'd catch up with me one of these days," he said feebly.

"You bastard," Jonse said coldly. "You killed my wife." It took effort to keep from kicking this face into a bloody pulp. "She didn't do anything to you."

"I know," The man said simply. His eyes were pleading with Jonse for understanding. "I didn't want to kill her," he said weakly. "But I had to. You see, she caught—'' His words were suddenly cut off, and a convulsion shook him before his body became rigid. His eyes went wide and staring, as his head fell limply to one side.

Jonse felt as though his legs would buckle. He realized then what a tremendous prop hatred could be. He shook his head. He didn't even know this man's name, but Jonse's reason for living had been bound up in that motionless form.

Jonse heard the sound of the front door opening, and he had to force his beaten muscles to turn toward the veranda. Sēnora Higuera was in the doorway, her eyes horror filled in a stricken face. She looked at the body, then at Jonse. Hate worked her mouth and put a new fire in her eyes.

''You killed him,'' she said shrilly. ''You shot him down.''

Manuel shoved at her to clear the doorway. ''Madre,'' he cried. ''Get out of my way.'' He struggled to push by her and raise the rifle he carried.

Jonse leveled his pistol at Manuel. ''Tell him to drop that rifle,'' he snapped. For a moment, it looked as though they didn't hear, or didn't want to.

''Damn you,'' Jonse yelled. ''You've lost one son. Another is wounded and in Marita's house. Maybe he won't make it. Do you want your third son killed?''

Manuel was almost by his mother, and he was raising the rifle muzzle. Jonse pointed the pistol at him. He didn't want to shoot this one, but if she didn't stop her son, Jonse would shoot.

Eulalia understood what Jonse said now, for her eyes turned sick, and her face crumpled into complete ruin. She grabbed Manuel's rifle barrel with both hands and struggled to pull it from his grip.

"Manuel," she screamed. "Drop it. He means what he say."

Some plea in her stricken eyes must have reached Manuel, for he let go of the rifle and let it fall to the ground.

The hollow spot in his stomach slowly filled. For a fleeting second, Jonse thought he would have to kill Manuel, too.

Jonse's rage returned, and he unleashed it on the woman. He jerked his head toward the dead man. "There's the killer you hired. You hated Marita so much, you couldn't stand her living close to you. Your killer murdered Pancho, the most harmless man I ever knew. Pancho's dog marked this killer. All I was trying to do was to see if Andras was so marked. But he lost his head— "Jonse shook his head, then said flatly, "He forced me to shoot him. Did you send Rafael after me?"

Eulalia rocked back and forth as she moaned, "I did not send him. I did not know he was gone until just a little while ago."

That was possible, Jonse conceded. If so, then a brother's grief for another had sent Rafael after him. "I didn't have to kill him," he said. "Though he is badly wounded. Despite what you did to Marita, she is taking care of your son."

He didn't say that Rafael would never be the same, nor did he speak of the personal reason he killed the man Señora Higuera hired. At the moment, neither of those things were important. In some way, he had to clear the poison out of this woman's mind, or it would go on and on until the ultimate tragedy stopped it all.

Manuel had withdrawn from his mother, and his

face was filled with horror. "You did all this?" he exclaimed incredulously.

"Manuel," she begged. "Don't you see? I did it for all of us."

Manuel shook his head, a slow, decisive gesture. "Not for all of us. Only you."

Señora Higuera was moaning now, sounding like an animal in mortal pain. This could be the breaking of that blind, arrogant spirit that pushed this woman to such measures. Her son's judgment might be just the thing to keep her in line. Jonse hoped so.

Señora Higuera twisted and pulled at her hands. "Could I see my son?" she asked, and all of the fire had gone out of her voice.

Marita might resent Eulalia's presence, and Jonse couldn't blame her for that. But he took it upon himself to say, "Marita would welcome you."

He expected some flash of passion to show how distasteful his words were to her, but she only nodded dully.

Manuel moved closer to his mother and put an arm about her shoulders. "We will be there soon."

"Good," Jonse said briskly. "Rafael might not be well enough to be moved for several days. I can promise you he will get the best of care until he is ready to travel."

"*Bueno*," Manuel said softly.

Jonse started to turn away, then a thought occurred to him. "Who was he?" he asked, indicating the body.

Manuel waited for his mother to speak. Jonse saw how hard it was for her to get those few words out. She wouldn't meet his eyes as she said, "I only knew him as Red Scurlock.'' She sought for a further explanation, and Jonse said quietly, ''It doesn't matter.''

Jonse walked to Ramon and mounted. Manuel raised a hand, and Jonse responded. There might never be friendship between these two branches of Higueras, but they could live together in peace. Jonse couldn't complain. This had turned out far better than he had any hope for.

He turned Ramon and headed down the long lane, never looking back.

Marita and Luis were outside to greet him when Jonse rode up to the house.

''*Dios* has answered my prayers,'' Marita said as she gripped his hand.

Jonse's grin was strong and true. ''It's all done, Marita. Lord, I'm tired.''

Luis took his other arm. Both of them were bursting with questions, but those could·be held for the moment.

''Come in and sit down,'' Luis said. ''Madre, is the coffee hot?''

''It will be soon,'' she responded.

Jonse knew a quick worry as he looked around the room. When he left, Rafael had been lying on the floor. He wasn't there now. Dear God, if he hadn't made it— He sucked in a hard breath. If Rafael had died, then the trouble could start all over again.

Marita understood the fear in Jonse's eyes, for she said, ''Luis and I moved him to a bed. He is sleeping. Each passing moment, he grows stronger.''

Jonse could grin again. ''Not seeing him scared the

hell out of me. I told Eulalia where he is. I took the privilege of telling her she was welcome to visit him until he can be moved.''

"She is welcome," Marita said without the slightest hesitation.

Jonse looked at her in wonder. She was quite a woman, incapable of holding hatred.

Jonse walked inside with them and sat down, stretching his long legs before him. He hadn't realized how thoroughly beaten he was until now.

He looked from one to the other. "It's done," he said quietly. "Señora Higuera is convinced she should no longer trouble you."

Neither of them spoke, but there was apprehension in their eyes. They wanted so badly to believe him, but they were afraid.

Jonse smiled at them. "I think this morning drove all the hate out of Eulalia, or at least dampened it so that she'll be able to forget you live here. She hired an American to run you two off your land. He was the one who killed Pancho. Lupe's teeth marked him well."

Marita closed her eyes, and Jonse thought she was praying.

Luis's face shown with a new eagerness. "What happened to him?"

Jonse looked at him in mild surprise. Luis shouldn't have to ask that. "I killed him," Jonse said simply.

There were tears in Marita's eyes when she reopened them. She brushed at them angrily and said, "Here I stand while you wait for your coffee."

Jonse smiled as she bustled around the stove. She

accepted a gift without the encumbrance of asking a lot of questions.

But Luis's curiosity was bubbling. He wouldn't be satisfied until he heard every detail. "Did you know him?"

"Too well." The harshness returned to Jonse's voice. "He was the one I was chasing when you found me that night. He killed my wife."

Luis's mouth opened, and he stared blankly at Jonse.

Marita left the stove. She came up to Jonse and placed a hand on his shoulder. "I am so sorry."

Jonse covered the hand. "I know," he said. He still felt empty inside, but the torment was fading. In time, he supposed he would know a sort of peace.

"*Dios* works in marvelous ways," Marita said. "Why He took from you, I will never know. But He sent you to us in our need."

Jonse nodded slowly. Maybe that was as good an answer as he would ever find.

"What will you do now?" Luis asked.

"Impose on you a week or two longer," Jonse replied. "I want to be sure Cribber and Streak are recovered enough to travel. Then I have to go home." The word "home" had a hollow ring. He had a house and property, but it would never again be really a home.

Marita's distress showed in her face and voice. "But you will come back soon."

"I might just do that," Jonse said slowly. "I never thought I could look at sheep with anything but a jaundiced eye. But Luis got me interested in them. I like the possibilities of profit in them. I just might come back and look around.''

"See," Marita said triumphantly. "The *bien Dios* thinks you will be an excellent sheepman. There is good land available not over twenty miles from here.''

Jonse wasn't ready to go so far as to agree with everything Marita said, but an idea was forming firmly in his mind. There were good people everywhere, but these two were special. If he was looking for a family he could claim, he could do no better.

"I'll sure do some thinking about it," he promised. He liked the happy look exchanged between Marita and Luis.

Marita gave Jonse's shoulder a final squeeze. "You asked for coffee, and here I stand gabbling away," she said in self-accusation. She whirled and hurried back to the stove.

Jonse felt an odd contentment steal through him. The first time he looked at Marita, he knew she was something out of the ordinary. A man's first impression could often be wrong. This time, it wasn't.